SPECIAL PAYMENTS

Johannesburg looks like any other thriving, prosperous metropolis. It's got the same crowds of brightly clad people swarming round the shops, the traffic, the stink of diesel fumes in the sweltering heat. It's got new underground shopping centres built in concrete, expensive restaurants, chic cocktail bars, big, plushy hotels, with hookers seated in the wide open foyers. On the face of it, Johannesburg is a sophisticated modern city with all the dubious delights of modern architecture that any city planning department could muster.

But behind the facade, beneath the new motorways that swirl round the city's heights, the glass tower blocks and the fountained squares, Johannesburg is a mining camp. It started life as a mining camp, it was built on the wealth of the gold mines that surround it. Its powerful mining houses and banks were born out of the profits of gold mining, and most of the people who run it are miners at heart.

SPECIAL PAYMENTS

Jeremy Woods

ARROW BOOKS

For G and G, with much love

Arrow Books Limited
17-21 Conway Street, London W1P 6JD

An imprint of the Hutchinson Publishing Group

London Melbourne Sydney Auckland
Johannesburg and agencies throughout
the world

First published by Hutchinson 1984
Arrow edition 1985

© Jeremy Woods 1984

Printed and bound in Great Britain by
Anchor Brendon Limited, Tiptree, Essex

ISBN 0 09 943780 5

'Throughout the detailed investigation that followed the arrests in New York, witnesses repeatedly expressed their belief that substantial sums of money changed hands as gifts, rewards or inducements. During this investigation, payments of this nature are referred to as "Special Payments".'

File Note – Securities Exchange Commission

I

Johannesburg
Monday 5 September
11.30 a.m.

Eddie Vandermeer sat at the oak leather-topped desk in the middle of his sixth-floor office, high above the swarming crowds and traffic on Hollard Street and directly across from the main entrance to the Johannesburg stock exchange.

The phones had stopped ringing for the first time that sunny spring morning and the silence gave Eddie a moment to think clearly through the crisis closing in around him.

Sitting there alone, sunlight pouring in through the window behind him, the warmth across his shoulders, Eddie experienced a new kind of fear. It was the quick panicky fear that comes with the shock of a large, unexpected financial loss.

In just under two hours, Eddie had plunged the respectable, medium-sized firm of stockbrokers Vandermeer & Vandermeer into its first ever financial crisis. It was his father's business, but now, after only two weeks under Eddie's care, Vandermeer & Vandermeer faced collapse.

He glanced down at the handwritten list of clients who had closed their accounts that morning. It contained the best names in Johannesburg's financial community. They were all there. The big banks, the insurance funds and the pension funds. They were names his father had worked hard all his life to represent.

The phone broke the silence.

'Vandermeer?' demanded a voice angrily.

'Edward Vandermeer speaking.'

'Are you the son of a bitch who wrote this crap about

gold? Well I want to tell you, I've never read such shit in all my life.'

'Who is this speaking?'

'Jock McCullough, chairman, Union Mining.'

For a moment it stunned him. Union Mining was the firm's largest client. Jock McCullough was legendary in South African mining circles. The McCullough children owned one of the many discretionary trusts that Eddie managed in his new job at Vandermeer & Vandermeer.

A dry 'Yes, sir' was all that he could manage for that moment.

'Let me tell you Mr Vandermeer,' continued McCullough, 'I am sick and tired of brokers like you trading our shares so they can cream off a nice fat commission each time.'

'Your children's trust is managed by us on a discretionary basis, Mr McCullough. If you don't want us to have discretion on dealing decisions, I'm sure we can manage the account differently.'

'Don't tell me how to run my business,' yelled McCullough. 'If I hadn't known your father all these years I'd close the account down now.'

There was sudden silence. McCullough was embarrassed at his outburst of temper, while Eddie contemplated losing the firm's biggest client.

'Jesus,' exclaimed McCullough, 'whores and stockbrokers are all the same. They'll screw you into the floor for a ten-rand note.'

Eddie tried to interrupt, but was shouted down.

'Listen to me goddammit. I phoned to tell your father, but as he's not there you'll do. If my kids lose a cent over this, you've bought and sold your last share for Union Mining or any of its associates. If you've cocked this up Vandermeer, you can kiss your arse goodbye.'

Before Eddie had a chance to answer, the line went dead. He was left sitting at his desk, phone in hand, the dial tone drilling loudly in his ear. He replaced the receiver and slumped back into his chair. Calls like that he could do without.

8

A strange, eerie, numbness spread across his body and the backs of his fingers started to tingle. He had been in trouble before, but somehow there had always been a way out. . . . Right now, he couldn't see any way at all.

Two weeks earlier, Eddie, at his father's request, had left his job as an investment analyst in London and made a triumphant return home to South Africa to take over the family business. Vandermeer & Vandermeer was one of the most prosperous and respected names on the Johannesburg stock exchange. Now, after only two weeks under Eddie's care, it was on a collision course with disaster. That list of names held the key. Over the years, Eddie's father had expanded Vandermeer's research department to attract the stockbroking business of the institutions. Vandermeer's now had the highest paid team of investment analysts in South Africa and could offer clients the best advice completely free.

The institutions responded. The solid flow of large orders they placed with Vandermeer & Vandermeer had become the life blood of the firm. Now the clients were disappearing fast and the blood was running thin.

A moment later Eddie added Union Mining to the list. Beside its name he put a question mark. The others had closed their accounts. There was a chance Union Mining might not.

Slowly, he read the names again. There were seven in all, Vandermeer's largest institutional clients, and together they accounted for over half Vandermeer & Vandermeer's annual turnover. He did not need to work out the figures, he knew the firm was in trouble. It would be impossible to replace clients of their size and power before the firm ran out of money. He reckoned he had four weeks at the most.

Eddie would have to tell his father; that would be the worst part. He wasn't worried for himself. He was a born dealer and had a strong instinct for survival. He had lived for years in the lush, turbulent foothills inhabited by many stockmarket dealers and had always accepted with a quiet sense of calm that the ultimate downside to many of his ventures was that he might, temporarily, be put out of business.

Apart from being a shrewd market operator, he was a handsome man in the best traditions of his Dutch ancestry – tall, blond, a finely featured face with deep blue eyes that glistened with a kind of icy detachment. He was intelligent and sensitive and had a natural, easy-going charm few people could resist.

But he had a weakness too, and it was a serious one that dominated a large part of his working life. Eddie loved to gamble. He was never reckless. The chances he took were always researched in depth and carefully calculated. But when he found a share that looked a certain winner he put his money, money borrowed from the bank against share certificates, and clients' money, into it. He never really knew when to stop. When it went up, there was no feeling of exhilaration like it; if it went down he almost enjoyed the challenge of getting everyone out safely. Most of the time his schemes paid off.

And at home he had his family. Eddie glanced across the desk at the photo of Lucy and the two girls sitting beside their pool, all three in their bikinis. Lucy was pretty, and tall like Eddie. She had long, black, straight hair, an oval-shaped face and round, slightly hooded eyes. There were many better-looking women, but few who had her vivacity and sense of fun. Each arm was wrapped around a wriggling, giggling little girl. Their sun-bleached blonde hair stood out against Lucy's dark skin and hair, and although there was nearly two years between them, the little girls could have passed for twins.

For a while Eddie gazed in front of him, focusing on nothing . . . lost in the flow of frightening thoughts that flared through his mind. Vandermeer & Vandermeer could be 'hammered' from the Johannesburg stock exchange, his family and father would be disgraced, and his career as an investment adviser would come to a short, traumatic end.

'Oh Jesus,' he sighed to himself.

This time he was stalked and cornered. This time he could see no way out. And his mind raced back to that

10

morning only two weeks earlier when he stepped out of the plane into the sunlight at Jan Smuts airport; the prodigal son returned, the golden boy of his father's dreams, come home to take over the family firm.

Eddie came back to South Africa with his own ideas about where to invest money. Michael Delaney, his boss at Cazenove, a leading London firm of stockbrokers where Eddie had worked for three years, had given him the clue over a farewell drink in a City wine bar.

Although they had worked closely together in the office, they had never really socialized and there was a slight hesitancy as they stood at the bar together.

'What'll you have?' asked the older man.

Eddie laughed. 'South African, of course!'

'Red?'

'Yes, let's try the Backsburg. I haven't had any for ages.'

'Right.'

Michael Delaney ordered the wine, paid for it, and poured two glasses.

'Well Eddie,' he said, raising his glass and giving the deep, red Backsburg a slight swirl. 'We'll miss you. Good luck.'

'Likewise Mike, I've enjoyed my time with you. Learnt a lot.'

Both men sipped their wine. Michael Delaney was a quiet, mild-mannered man in his late fifties, who had been head of the Cazenove research department ever since Eddie joined the firm. He knew Eddie's father from the war years, when they had both served in the same tank regiment, and had taught Eddie most of what he knew about investment analysis.

'You know Eddie, you're going back to an interesting country. The Americans can't go on ignoring their budget deficit much longer. They have to borrow $80 billion a year just to finance it – the country's living on borrowed money and the dollar is living on borrowed time.'

'But they could do something about it,' countered Eddie. 'All the major markets are moving up.'

'Don't trust it, Eddie. It can't last. Right now, the hardship measures involved in cutting the deficit are politically unacceptable. So they're stuck with a soaring deficit, high interest rates, and a pumped up dollar.'

'Not to mention South America,' added Eddie. 'If Brazil, or any of them, decided not to repay their loans, it could cause havoc to the American banking system.'

Michael Delaney moved a little closer and Eddie watched his calm, intelligent eyes.

'They can wallpaper the effects of South America, but sooner or later they are going to have to tackle the deficit. If they try to cut it with tight monetary control, economic growth stops in its tracks, the dollar plunges and interest rates soar to protect it. Net result – you get another bout of inflation.'

'Investors panic, sell industrials and buy gold,' said Eddie.

'Right. You've got the message. If gold is good South Africa is good. You could be moving at the right time.'

Eddie had not forgotten the conversation. He thought about it during most of the eleven-hour flight from London to Johannesburg. By the time he reached South Africa, it was part of his new investment philosophy. Buy gold, sell industrials.

He took a week to settle into his new job as dealing partner and spent most of it in the bars and restaurants around Hollard Street meeting Vandermeer & Vandermeer's clients.

His new job was to manage the firm's large number of discretionary portfolios as well as oversee Vandermeer's dealing operation in the stockmarket.

The first thing Eddie did once he had settled in was to catalogue the various portfolio holdings into mining,

12

financial, and industrial shares and then calculate their market worth. To his surprise, he found the portfolios had a market value in excess of R60 million, 80 per cent of which was invested in blue chip industrials. This was a situation Eddie viewed with grave concern. He consulted his father one evening over dinner. William Vandermeer had his reservations, but he respected Michael Delaney's investment views and did not want to stifle his son's enthusiasm so early on in their new working relationship. He knew Eddie was ambitious to make a name for himself on the Johannesburg stockmarket and he wanted to give him full rein to do so. He had never taken bold investment decisions like this, but he went along with it. The firm's discretionary clients would be switched out of industrials into gold. But first, Eddie agreed to set his views out in an investment letter for all Vandermeer & Vandermeer's clients.

It was a shocker. Entitled 'The Over-Riding Case for Gold', it concluded, ' . . . we believe the major investment decision of the moment is not *whether* industrials shares should be sold, but *how quickly* they can be sold.'

At 3.00 p.m. on Friday 22 September, just as business on the Johannesburg stock exchange was winding down for the weekend, a wave of selling hit top industrials right across the board. The *Rand Daily Mail* index of industrial shares, which had showed a gain of 4.5 points on the day's trading, had plunged 18 points by the close.

At 3.35 p.m. Eddie's head dealer called to say all the sales had been completed. Eddie had stayed in his room back at the office. He thought his presence in the market when his firm was doing all the selling might have caused undue alarm. Dealing partners in the big firms rarely go on the trading floor to deal. They issue instructions and leave it to their dealing staff to carry them out.

The operation had gone well: 'By the time the boys woke up to what was happening, most of them had enough stock to give them indigestion for a month,' his head dealer told him.

That night the entire client list of Vandermeer & Vandermeer were posted Eddie's first investment advice letter to his new clients. The discretionary clients also received individually written letters explaining that in accordance with the advice contained in the newsletter, most of their industrial shares had been sold and the proceeds reinvested in leading long-life gold mines.

Driving home that evening to the plush northern suburbs, Eddie leant out of the driving seat window of the blue Porsche Targa Sports, and hummed quietly across the stereo. The evening sky was clear and blue and the musky scent of spring flowers drifted across the motorway in the warm evening air.

2

The calls started at 8.30 a.m. the following Monday morning as soon as Eddie arrived at his desk. Some clients were abusive. Many, like McCullough, he had never even met. They came from the largest pension fund to the smallest investors. It was the most depressing two hours in Eddie's 33-year-old life.

To make matters worse, the *Rand Morning Mail*, South Africa's biggest circulation daily newspaper, picked up the story. The city editor in his 'Money Talks' column heralded the newsletter as 'the latest oddball view from a respectable firm of stockbrokers'. It started: 'There is always someone prepared to stick their neck out in the interests of more business and try to call the top of a bull market. The latest attempt from Vandermeer & Vandermeer is less than convincing. . . .'

By 10.00 a.m. the Johannesburg stockmarket had recouped most of its late Friday collapse. The disgruntled institutional investors who had bought heavily on Friday, kicked their heels in glee and stepped back into the market as aggressive buyers.

At the 11.00 a.m. reading, the industrial market was up 19.6 points, its largest one-day rise in two years. The gold market was quiet and dull, with persistent small sales depressing prices. Eddie sat at his desk pondering his position. He would have to tell his father. William Vandermeer had all the newspapers delivered to his office during the week, so he could sit quietly for half an hour before the market opened and digest the morning's financial and economic news. Eddie knew he would have heard by now if his father had seen the story. He glanced at his watch. It was 11.30 a.m. The old man had left his house at 7.30 a.m. that morning and stopped off at the surgery on his way into work for a medical check.

Now sixty-eight years old, William Vandermeer had suffered a heart attack the previous year. His steadily deteriorating health was the main reason Eddie had returned to South Africa.

Eddie walked over to the window and stared out across the rooftops of the offices across the street to the tower blocks and hotels that had sprung up around the city. For him there was no other city like Johannesburg; none of them had the same feel, that same naked pulse. To those who don't know it, Johannesburg looks like any other thriving, prosperous metropolis. It's got the same crowds of brightly clad people swarming round the shops, the traffic, the stink of diesel fumes in the sweltering heat. It's got new underground shopping centres built in concrete, expensive restaurants, chic cocktail bars, big, plushy hotels, with hookers seated in the wide open foyers. On the face of it, Johannesburg is a sophisticated modern city with all the dubious delights of modern architecture that any city planning department could muster.

But behind the facade, beneath the new motorways that swirl round the city's heights, the glass tower blocks and the fountained squares, Johannesburg is a mining camp. It started life as a mining camp, it was built on the wealth of the gold mines that surround it. Its powerful mining houses and banks were born out of the profits of gold mining, and most of the people who run it are miners at heart.

Eddie looked down for his father's car among the three

lanes of traffic grinding noisily down the street, but couldn't see it.

The pavements were crammed with a seething mass of pedestrians side-stepping each other as they sped up and down Hollard Street. Most of them were associated with the Johannesburg stock exchange.

There were dealers from the house floor, brokers, secretaries, clients. They bustled up and down in front of the main entrance to the stock exchange with an urgency not found half a mile down Hollard Street around the city's retail heart, the Carlton Centre.

The green Mercedes saloon drew up against the kerb below the office window. Eddie watched as France, the firm's black driver, sprang out and opened the back door. But he knew better than to help William Vandermeer onto the street.

The old man pulled himself out of the car, one hand gripping the top of the rear door, straightened himself up on his stick, and stood waiting to cross the pavement towards the ground-floor entrance to his office.

Eddie watched him. His shoulders were slightly stooped and his cane walking stick, essential since the last heart attack, was held out unsteadily to cut a passage through the fast-moving crowds. For a while no one stopped for him, and he stood on the edge of the pavement frail and helpless. Then France, careful not to give any direct assistance, cut a passage through the people with an outstretched arm.

Eddie dreaded telling his father the bad news. All his working life had been spent building the business and reputation of Vandermeer & Vandermeer. The disgrace and humiliation of being 'hammered' from the Johannesburg stock exchange was a disaster his father, in his present condition, might not survive. It was this that troubled Eddie more than anything else.

3

Minutes later Eddie knocked quietly on the oak-panelled door to his father's office and walked in. William Vandermeer looked up and signalled him into a chair. He was talking on the telephone. Deep concern lit the old man's grey eyes and his voice was slow and serious.

'Jock, we have been friends too long to let a thing like this come between us. I know how you feel, and if we change the portfolio again, it will only be with your full consultation and agreement.'

He raised his eyebrows to Eddie and drew his right hand quickly across his throat gesturing mock execution.

'Yes, I'll talk to Eddie. He's just walked into my office. We'll hold the gold shares for three months. If there's no movement by then we'll put your children back into industrials.' He smiled and his voice became relaxed and expansive. 'If your kids lose money – I'll take it straight out of Eddie's salary.'

The old man put the phone down and eased himself back into the swivel chair, holding the piece of paper he had scribbled notes on. He was about to speak when Eddie held up his hands.

'Don't tell me. Jock McCullough. If I lose his kids a cent, no more business.' His father nodded.

'He called me earlier. He wasn't quite so polite, but there was no doubt about the message.'

'You know what the loss of the Union Mining account would mean to this firm, Eddie. It's our largest client, and Jock McCullough has been a friend of mine since our school days together. Right now, he's as mad as hell.'

The old man spoke slowly. His face was clear and bright, but he had lost weight since the heart operation. The brown, wrinkled skin was stretched a little tighter across his cheeks and jaw, and Eddie noticed new lines and wrinkles had aged his gaunt face.

He was a small, compact man with a shock of meticulously combed white hair. He still looked dapper in his blue, sea-island cotton shirts and grey lightweight suits. But once or twice in the past two weeks Eddie had noticed the focus of his eyes was a little more distant, and his gaze a fraction more remote. Just for a moment he saw it again.

'Dad, the clients are going mad about my switch into gold. Jock McCullough's just one: There're another half-dozen banks and pension funds screaming blue murder and threatening to close down their accounts.'

The old man sat and listened impassively.

'There's not one of them got the guts or the foresight to get into the gold market. I'm still confident we're right,' said Eddie. 'But I can't convince the clients. The bastards think the industrial market is going up for ever.'

Eddie opened the newspaper and laid it in front of his father.

'While we're on the subject – you'd better read this.' The old man read the article without a word.

'Eddie, you can't blame yourself. I read what you wrote and approved the share sales. Who has closed their accounts?'

'Bank of South Africa, Rand Bank, Liberty Assurance . . .'

'OK . . . OK. I've known those people all my life. Give them a day to cool down and I'll talk to them. And I'll talk to the solicitors about the piece in the paper. The idea we're touting for business with oddball ideas is the last sort of publicity we need right now.'

William Vandermeer leant back into his swivel chair, straightened his back, and paused for a moment's reflection.

'I think our real problem is not what has happened so far – it's a storm in a teacup and we can patch it up – but what might happen in the weeks ahead. If you're wrong about the gold market, these people lose money. If gold stands still and the industrial market keeps going up, they could lose a lot.'

'I still feel the same. Any way I look at it, corporate

profits are going to take a beating over the next nine months. If I'm wrong, I'll resign.'

His father nodded, lifted himself from his chair and walked uncertainly across the office to open the door.

'I've spent my life building this business Eddie. I don't want to see it thrown away.'

'Dad, don't worry. I'll get us out of it. I'm not throwing anything away.'

Eddie felt strangely angry and rebellious. He pushed his chair back roughly and stood up to leave. As he walked past his father, the old man took his arm.

'I trust you son, and I have confidence in your views. But just remember, if you're wrong, there may not be much of a firm left to resign from.'

4

Every day for the next three days the price of gold fell heavily. It dropped $13 an ounce the first day, $17 the following day, and plunged through the important psychological support level of $400 an ounce the third day with a $22 drop to $396.

For Eddie, the sudden slide and final sell-off at the bottom of a bear market came as no surprise. He had not expected it to be so sharp. He had not expected it at exactly that time. But he always knew there would be a sell-off, as there is at the bottom of every market. And this one was a textbook classic.

There was no fundamental economic reason for the fall. There wasn't even any heavy selling. But the steady drip of small sales onto a nervous market kept the price of gold in the main trading centres, New York and London, on a steady downward trend.

The weakness brought out short-sellers in force and the whole nasty little movement gathered momentum into a sharp gold price collapse.

It sparked a wave of panic selling in the gold market,

which, after three devastating days, left gold shares 20 per cent lower across the board.

Once again the complaining phone calls started. For three days Eddie sat at his desk in a state of siege. He argued his case to exhaustion. He was cross-questioned, insulted, and, by Friday lunchtime, was starting to lose his voice.

The Johannesburg stock exchange closed quietly at 3.30 p.m. that Friday afternoon, the first bank holiday weekend of official summertime. Some of the dealers had left the market after lunch. By the close, the offices of Vandermeer & Vandermeer were deserted.

Eddie walked into the main office making his routine security patrol before going home. He sat broodily on the side of a desk and surveyed the lines of empty desks and telephones. Over in one corner the wire service machines chattered out the local closing prices and final reports on the day's trading. He rubbed the side of his neck. His glands were up and his throat sore. Perhaps his clients were right. Perhaps he was too young, too impetuous. . . . Among the local investment community he was a minority of one – and those are dangerous odds for a financial adviser.

The phone rang on a desk across the room. With sinking heart he picked up the receiver.

'Eddie?' said his wife Lucy. 'What are you doing on the switchboard?'

'The way things look here, most of our clients think its the only job I'm qualified for,' he smiled.

'Ah! You and that stockmarket,' she sighed. 'You know you love it really.'

'Right now, you can keep it.'

'Darling,' she said, changing the subject, 'the girls and I have packed the camper and I'm just about to light the barbecue for supper. When will you be home?'

'I'm leaving now.'

In the turmoil he had forgotten he promised Lucy the long weekend away camping in the Lesotho mountains. He glanced quickly around the office, grabbed his briefcase and took the lift down to the gleaming new Porsche in the basement. Twenty minutes later, he turned off the motorway at the Houghton exit and headed for home.

Turning into his driveway, he saw the Volkswagen camper packed and waiting in front of the house, while across by the pool the barbecue flamed in the early evening stillness.

Suddenly, the two girls, Sarah and Rachel, came running out of the house and down the driveway towards him, waving and shouting.

He unbuttoned the top of his shirt and loosened his tie. It was time to stop worrying about the gold price, at least until after the holiday.

5

They left the house the next day at 4.30 a.m. while dawn was breaking.

As the loaded camper trundled slowly down the drive in the early morning half-light, Lucy noticed the lights going on in the servant's quarters. Josiah and his wife Emily had been with her family for fifteen years. They had brought her up almost singlehanded, and now ran the house like clockwork whether she was there or not.

Lucy settled back into the front seat of the camper, sleepy but content. Her parents had moved into the guest wing for the weekend. The two girls, tucked up in their beds, would be safe and well cared for. As much as she loved her kids, it was a treat to have her husband away from the office and all to herself.

She sat curled up as the camper sped through the deserted freeway system of Johannesburg. She yawned quietly to herself gazing aimlessly out at the jagged, black shadows of office buildings stretched out across the freeway. A yellow rim of light broke a line through the darkened horizon before her.

'Still tired, darling?' asked Eddie.

'I'm fine,' she murmured.

She shifted across the bench seat, slipped an arm around his shoulders and rested her head lightly on his shoulder. How she still loved him. Most of her friends were either divorced, having affairs, or just plain bored with their men. She always felt slightly embarrassed when they talked about it. Her own marriage was quite different. She loved Eddie and did not dare think how she would cope without him.

It was light now and the sun was starting to climb. Lucy poured some coffee from a thermos and they both sipped at it in silence.

The first hundred kilometres out of Johannesburg in any direction are flat and boring. The farm lands of the Transvaal stretched out before them, a vast agricultural patchwork of wheat, maize and barley fields. Occasionally, they passed fields of sunflowers, the long lines of plants stretching for miles along the roadside, their great yellow heads bowed.

The string of one-horse towns that dotted across the fertile plains of the Platteland, from Johannesburg to the rolling hills of Natal, are all pretty much the same. Pitzberg, Heidelberg, Krantz and Welcom are typical Platteland towns and strong bastions of the Afrikaans way of life. They are rarely more than one house deep along the main highway and have a hotel with a bar, a supermarket, a general store and a garage that often doubles as a farm machinery depot. They are farming towns where the harsh, guttural Afrikaans tongue of the Boers is the daily language. Few shopkeepers will speak English – even to passing English-speaking tourists. It's not that they can't – they just won't.

Soon the flat plains of the Platteland started to undulate gently. Then suddenly, there in the distance were the unmistakable green foothills of the magnificent Blue Mountain range. They rose out of the land like a landscape from a children's fairy tale. The peaks were snow-capped and the mountains stood out blue and grey in the morning light.

* * *

From the position of their camp high up in the Blue Mountains on a flat plateau of grass beside the Singunyana river, Eddie gazed at the spectacular panorama of mountains that stretched out in front of him as far as the eye could see. The heat had gone out of the early evening sun and the peaks before him were touched by a fiery red wash as the sun slid behind the mountains.

Eddie sat beside the newly made fire, rocking to and fro in an old, army-surplus canvas chair. He sipped from a large glass of cold white wine. The day's sunburn prickled his body and his skin felt tight from swimming in the river.

The fire jumped and spluttered in the early evening stillness and the smell of pine and smoke drifted round the camp. An old barbecue grill sat across the flames sizzling and smoking while behind the camp was the quiet roar of the fast-flowing Singunyana river. Lucy worked in the back of the camper preparing food for the barbecue. They fell quite naturally into the same routine when they were camping. Eddie found the wood and lit the fire. Lucy organized the food, and they barbecued it together.

Eddie drained his glass and refilled it. Then he lit another cigarette and inhaled deeply. The sun had sunk out of sight leaving a blaze of crimson stretched across the horizon against the now darkened outline of the Blue Mountains.

It had been a good day. The best he could remember for a long time. They had driven into Maseru, the colourful, shanty-town capital of Lesotho early that morning, and headed straight out to the mountains. After a gruelling two-hour drive up a steep, heavily rutted mountain road, they made camp beside the Singunyana, a river fed straight from the melting snowcaps above them.

They climbed up through the pine-clad mountainside that towered above their camp in the morning, drank wine by the river at lunchtime, and fell asleep under a clump of trees on the river bank during the heat of the afternoon. When Eddie awoke he was hot and his head throbbed from too much alcohol. He pulled off his clothes and waded into the fast, swirling waters of the Singunyana. Swimming over to a long, sturdy branch overhanging the river, Eddie grabbed it with both hands and let his body float with the flow of the icy water. Closing his eyes, he put his mind at rest and let his senses soak up the sensation.

He held on till his arms ached to be free, and then swam strongly to the river bank. It was always the same in these Lesotho mountains. They had a special effect, a serenity of their own. After just one day he felt much better – replenished and cleansed, and completely at one with his surroundings.

Lucy walked over to the table beside the fire and placed a plate of cleaned trout and chicken on it ready to barbecue. Then she sat on a canvas chair beside Eddie.

'Well,' she said jauntily, 'are we going to be bankrupted, disgraced and penniless – all at the same time?' It was the first time she had mentioned Eddie's business affairs since they left Johannesburg.

He grimaced. 'Maybe we'll have to set up permanent camp right here.'

Having broached the subject at last, Lucy felt more able to talk about it.

'So what if the price of gold goes through the floor? So what if Vandermeer's loses its clients? We had nothing when we started. We can always start again.'

Eddie put his arm round her and drew her closer to him.

'It's not us so much. I'm sure we'll be all right. It's Dad. He's spent his whole life building up the business and I've screwed it up in three weeks. If Vandermeer's goes under, I think he would go with it.'

'Your father is a lot tougher than you give him credit for. I'm sure he'd be far more worried to know you didn't fool around with your kids any more. You never seem to notice me. And we haven't made love for weeks.'

'Is that true?' he said turning towards her quickly.

She smiled and nodded slowly, a veil of embarrassment in her eyes. 'I don't mind. I understand how difficult things have been lately. But I think you miss a lot with the children. They're at an enchanting age and you're missing

24

it all because you're too worried to sit down and enjoy them.'

Eddie thought about what she said. He knew it was true. There was no answer. 'Come on. Let's eat. I'm starving.'

Lucy had prepared a feast. They barbecued the trout and chicken, jacket potatoes and onions on the fire together and drank wine from a gallon bottle while they ate. By the time they had finished, it was dark and only the flames from the fire lit the camp.

Later, Eddie unrolled the large, quilted sleeping bag and laid it beside the fire. The hills were wrapped in the thick, black, velvet of the African night and only the streams and rivers cascading down from the melting peaks broke the silence.

They lay in their sleeping bag, arms around each other, gazing up at the blue-starred African night sky.

Then Eddie felt the warmth of her lips upon his and the hardness of her nipples against his chest. They made love by the fire, the quiet thunder of the river in their ears, the glow of the embers on their faces. As the fire burnt down, they drifted off into sleep.

Across the other side of the world, fourteen hours flying time away in New York, it was 6 a.m. the following Monday morning. And that same sun was hauling itself up through the swirling, wet fog across Manhattan's waterfront and its first weak rays flickered over a clutch of glass-tinted skyscrapers on Wall Street. They housed the big banks and bullion dealers that make up the New York bullion market, the largest gold market in the world. While Eddie slept, the New York gold market was going to have a day few of the professional punters would forget for a long time.

6

New York
Monday 12 September
11.30 a.m.

Pierre Bouchard, the handsome 34-year-old Frenchman in charge of the bullion-dealing department of the Federal Union Bank's New York office sat in his office in one corner of the dealing room scanning the television screen at the end of his desk.

The gold market was dead. Dealers lounged around each other's desks drinking coffee and talking; it had been the same dreary mid-morning scene for the last ten weeks. Continual small selling from private investors depressing the market with the occasional big selling order from a central bank knocking the price down into new low ground.

Pierre had seen the trading pattern at least a dozen times before and was sure he would see it a dozen times again.

But now suddenly he sensed the atmosphere was changing. Earlier that morning the bank's management had decided to off-load a short term trading position of 25,000 ounces – some $10–million worth of gold – onto the market ahead of some bad, but already discounted, trade figures.

Pierre instructed his dealers, and by careful selling in one- and two-thousand ounce parcels, they sold off over half the amount and hardly disturbed the price. It stuck stoically at $398. Then it started to go against him, edging up to $401. Immediately he halted all sales and retreated quickly to his office.

Pierre had a sixth sense for impending action in the gold market and his antennae were picking up warning signals from this sudden demand for gold as he checked his Reuters terminal for news from the world's main trading centres.

Pierre was a dedicated competitor in the gold market and his uncanny ability to foresee the short-term runs and falls in the bullion price had led to his rapid promotion through the ranks. The bank had rarely been caught on the wrong foot or been put unnecessarily at risk. It was a record Pierre was proud of, and one he had every intention of keeping intact.

He turned, tapped out another code on the console and his eyes flicked back to the screen. The Zurich gold market report flashed onto the screen.

'Gold is trading quietly between $398 and $400. A trickle of small sales are coming onto the market but these are being absorbed by European bank purchases,' he read quickly.

He tapped out another code on the console. It was the same story in London. Small buying and selling, but no sign of any volume. Pierre raced through the figures, the fingers of his right hand tapping nervously across the flat, plastic top of the console.

Nothing in Europe, he thought. It must be local.

He glanced out through the glass partition separating his office from the dealing room. His dealers were at their desks, jackets off, shirt sleeves rolled, ties loosened, urgently answering their telephones. At least six switchboards were flashing red lights for waiting calls, some of the dealers were holding two phones.

Pierre moved quickly. He felt that strange tingling excitement creep into his body.

'Buy! Buy!' he shouted to the dealers as he ran out of his office. The dealing room hubbub stopped for an instant, then pandemonium broke out around the dealing desk. At each transaction the amount and price of the purchase was shouted out and Pierre jotted it down on a paper pad.

In the minutes it took to buy his 12,500 ounces of gold back the price jumped from just under $400 an ounce to $412. Piere's average price was $409. It's a terrifyingly fast game and there are times when all you have to play with is instinct.

'Support the market, let me know if the price comes off,' he told his head dealer.

If the price dropped to $380 he wasn't going to look terribly clever.

Pierre went back to the Reuters terminal in his office.

27

He pressed a button on the console and waited for a list of the day's financial headlines to appear. On the foreign exchange, the dollar was down on the day but trading had so far been light.

He punched out further instructions and the latest stock-market report from the New York stock exchange spread out across the screen. As he read, a newsflash appeared at the bottom of the screen.

'Prices are starting to fall heavily across the board after publication of the latest trade figures. Investors are worried by the latest rise in America's budget deficit, a two per cent jump in the monthly inflation rate and reports of a coup in Brazil by the Marxist Workers' Revolutionary Party. . . .'

Pierre whistled lightly. So that was it; someone had seen the trade figures. He spoke to his secretary through the intercom on his desk.

'Gill, please get these people fast in this order.' He gave her a list of Swiss bankers, New York bankers, his London stockbroker, and a handful of his own personal clients.

Then he checked the bank's bullion position on the computer terminal on the other side of his desk. It showed the bank had started the morning with a short-term trading position of 25,000 ounces of gold which had been reduced to 12,000 ounces. The latest purchases to reverse that situation were not shown yet.

He quickly wrote out a sale receipt to himself for 500 ounces of gold at $412.00 and knocked 500 ounces off his trading position. Then he wrote out a personal cheque for $206,000 pinned it to a copy invoice of the transaction and tossed it into his secretary's 'out' tray. He did so in the full and relaxed knowledge that if he kept the position open and his bank cashed the cheque, the money was there to meet it.

The first call arrived.

'Frank Larson, Union Bank,' said Gill and switched him through.

'Frank. What's the price and size of the market?'

As he spoke, Pierre checked the gold price on Reuters – it was up another $6 – then back through the Foreign Exchange market and the New York stockmarket. Industrial share prices were falling fast, and judging by the price of the last two trades, the dollar looked as though it was going into a tail-spin.

'It's $420, up to 20,000 ounces, Pierre.'

'That's $2 above the price here.'

'Take it or leave it, I'm afraid.'

'I'll take it,' replied Pierre. In the current buying spree locally, he knew his chances of getting any kind of size were slim.

'And another 20,000?'

'Another two,' said the flat detached voice with only a tremor of inquiry, 'will be $422.'

'I'll have them,' said Pierre.

Business over, the tone of voice at the other end became warmer and more friendly.

'Bad trade figures, eh Pierre?'

'Bad everything. Inflation. South America.'

'Then we'll see some action.'

'Don't go short Frank – our phones haven't stopped since the announcement, and the business is high quality.'

As soon as he put down the telephone, Frank Larsen dialled the bullion sales department of the South African Reserve Bank and arranged for his bank to take physical delivery of one ton of gold from stock.

By the time Pierre had safeguarded the bank's position, and looked after his own, there were more calls.

First was Pierre's boss and senior director on the board, Tertius Geron. Pierre reported his dealing manoeuvres and the current size and price of his trading book while he continued to rap out the codes for the latest prices on the foreign exchange, the stockmarket and the bullion market.

'Gold is now trading at $417.50,' he read from the screen.

He glanced out at the dealing room and the frenetic activity around the dealing desk.

'Tertius, we're getting very busy down here, I must go.'

'OK, Pierre, I'll be down shortly. Keep me in touch.'

In the next four minutes, six calls went through to Pierre. The first was his London stockbroker, Cazenove. He bought £50,000 worth of South African gold mining shares for himself 'at best'.

The next four were friends he advised privately, wealthy investors that Pierre had met over the years. They were used to these calls. Each year for the last three, Pierre had doubled the portions of their portfolios that they allowed him to trade in the gold market.

First one was Eddie Vandermeer's office in Johannesburg. The two had met in Johannesburg when Pierre worked for the family firm. Two years later when Pierre became a bullion dealer in London for one of the merchant banks, they met up again and became close friends.

'He's away for the weekend,' Pierre's secretary told him.

'All right. I'll book five hundred ounces to his Basle account, but remind me to call him in the morning.'

Eddie kept his bullion dealings out of the country as South African citizens are prohibited by law from dealing in gold. Pierre had instructions to take a position for him if he felt the price was going to move. The rest of the four bought stock outright.

He wrote out the orders, adjusted the gold tally, and left his desk to check his dealers.

'Looks good,' proffered his small, neat, Swiss head dealer.

'Any big buying?'

'Yes, but they're all within their dealing limits.'

He walked across to the dealing desk. Each of his dealers were talking on the telephone. As one call finished, they

30

immediately switched to another. Pierre listened for a moment to the clamour of the voices. On quiet days, the room could be almost silent.

By midday, the price of gold in New York and London had jumped to $421.00, the Dow Jones index had dropped 26 points and the value of the dollar had plummeted against most currencies on the world foreign exchange markets.

Around the bullion desk at Federal. Union, New York, the pace was hectic as news of the calamitous trade figures were absorbed by fund managers around the world.

Three times Pierre Bouchard went into the open market and bought sizeable amounts of gold. Three times his bank sold them at a profit.

The pressure for gold eased up over the lunch hour, but when those ever present Hong Kong dealers came in at 3.30 p.m. New York time, they deal around the clock in Hong Kong – the whole roller coaster started up again. Few investors gamble like the Chinese and by four o'clock Pierre was on the phone again to Zurich as gold hit $442 an ounce on the New York gold market – up 43 dollars on the day.

At 7.30 p.m. that evening when the other major institutions up and down Wall Street had switched out their lights and gone home, the third and fourth floor dealing rooms at Federal Union were still ablaze.

Two hours later, Pierre Bouchard stood on the street below waiting for a taxi to take him to his young French wife at home in their West Side apartment overlooking Central Park. His head throbbed, his eyes were sinking into his head with tiredness, and his neck and spine ached with tension.

When the taxi arrived, he threw himself into the back seat, gave his address and fell asleep for the fifteen-minute drive across the city.

It wasn't until he lay soaking in the bath, a large glass of Grand Cru Chablis in one hand, that he started to reflect on his dealing positions. He was $15,000 up on his bullion position, at least another $10,000 up on the gold shares

31

and the bank had made a killing. But what really brought a smile to his face, as he lay in the hot, soapy bath sipping wine, was the thought of the action to come. With the budget deficit swelling each month and inflation hitting new highs, the bullion market would be blazing for weeks.

7

Johannesburg
Tuesday 13 September
7 a.m.

Eddie was always glad to be home. Like his black servant, he woke up each morning as soon as it got light. He always made sure of a few minutes of solitude before the boy delivered the morning paper.

It was a sacred part of the day. No noise, no interruptions. His family were tucked up asleep in bed. He walked out onto the balcony overlooking the garden. The grass was heavy with spring dew and a thin mist lingered over the pool where the heat from the water met the cool morning air. The sun was just starting to climb, and though there was no appreciable heat from it yet, the soft light bathed the garden.

Eddie walked down the balcony steps to inspect his roses. About half the blooms were out now. The thick perfume from the deep red heads was overwhelming in the thin, clear air. He bent down, cupped a hand round one of the blooms and smelt the rich, musky bouquet. White spiders' webs were stretched between branches and the crimson petals were bowed with heavy droplets of moisture.

He strolled over to the pool and tested the temperature. Then slipped off his dressing gown and waded into the shallow end. The water felt deliciously warm, and he swam six lengths of lazy breast stroke before he heard the paper boy's cycle crunching down the driveway, and the creak of the post-box door as he pulled it open and slotted the paper inside.

Eddie lifted himself out of the pool, dried quickly, and pulling his dressing gown on, trotted across the lawn to get the paper. He had not seen or heard any financial news since he left the office on Friday night, and was keen to catch up on Monday's trading in the markets.

He pulled the paper out of the box, flicked it open and scanned the front page. The *Rand Morning Mail* sported the usual horror stories – an air crash in Madrid, more riots in Soweto and another South African raid into Angola.

Instinctively, he pulled out the business section. He read the headlines once. Then again, to make sure. He glanced through the main body of the story and then read it again.

'Gold leaps $43 on US trade figures.' He felt the excitement surge.

The price of bullion leapt forty-three dollars to $442 yesterday amid hectic dealings in New York and European financial centres after publication of the latest US trade figures. In New York the dollar fell to a new low and the Dow Jones Industrial Index fell by forty-two points, the biggest one-day drop since President Kennedy's assassination in 1963.

Eddie checked his watch. It was 7.15 a.m. His father would be awake now. He ran into the house, snatched the telephone and dialled.

'Dad, did you see the gold price yesterday?' he shouted.

'Yes, Eddie.' his father's voice was distinctly drowsy. 'I tried to call you last night, but you were home too late. I left a message with the girls.'

'They were asleep when we came in.'

'Well son, it was quite an exciting day. All the gold shares shot ahead and I was getting some sizeable orders from institutions I haven't spoken to for six months or more.'

'How strong was the local buying?'

'By the afternoon very strong, considering our market was closed. There was very little stock on offer in New York and some of the good mines made sizeable gains.'

'I hope you didn't sell any of our clients' shares, Dad?'

'None. As a matter of fact, I had McCullough on the phone jumping up and down for me to buy some more for his own account and his kids' trust.'

'That son of a bitch.'

'I checked with analysts in New York and London and they are worried inflation is getting out of control in the US. I phoned our brokers in Hong Kong just before I went to bed and the market was going mad over there. Gold was trading much higher that it closed in New York. You know what the Chinese are like when they get the bit between their teeth.'

'OK, Dad. Sorry to call you so early. I'm going to the office now. I'll see you later.'

By 7.45 that morning Eddie was sitting at his desk shaved, showered and dressed for the office in a white shirt and navy suit. He had picked up a toasted ham sandwich on the way in for breakfast, and made coffee on arrival. He sat at his desk drinking coffee between bites.

First he laid the entire previous day's tickertape across his desk in strips and studied them item by item. This told him how the day had progressed.Then he checked individual share prices. Some of the rises had been impressive for one day's trading. Most of the heavyweight gold shares were up by 10 per cent, while many of the low-grade gold mines, the marginal ones, had increased by more. His father had been right. The New York market must have been very short of stock. When a market had been falling for as long as the gold price had, there were very few punters prepared to hold stock on the way down.

Having checked the share prices, Eddie now turned to his discretionary portfolios. He picked his twelve largest clients and, with his calculator, worked out the trading profit so far on each one.

Finally, ten minutes before the official office opening time, he went into the post room to check the closing price of gold in Hong Kong. It was up another $7 to $449.

Hong Kong is a market that trades when other gold markets are asleep. It is an important market as the Far East is a big buyer of gold. Much of the gold bought in Hong Kong ends up in India where it adorns the ears, necks and wrists of the Indian women, and represents a family's fortune.

At 8 a.m. Eddie started to ring round his investment clients. The first call was to Union Mining and Jock McCullough. His secretary put Eddie through.

'McCullough,' said a flat, disinterested voice when the phone was picked up.

'Edward Vandermeer here. I know how upset you were when I bought gold shares for your children's discretionary trust. This call was just to say . . .'

'Just to say I fucking well told you so,' interrupted McCullough. There was silence for a few seconds, then McCullough laughed. 'You're right to ring young fella. I'd do just the same. Eddie, it's time we had a drink together. Come over to my office at 12.30. I'd like you to meet some of my fund managers. Stay for lunch.'

Eddie hesitated. He had never met Jock McCullough and remembered his phone call. Why not? he thought. He'll probably give me some business to make up for it.

'I'll be there,' he said.

'And Eddie,' said McCullough as he was about to put down the phone. 'Don't sell any. After yesterday – I'm a buyer.'

8

As much as he was looking forward to lunch with Jock McCullough, Eddie found it hard to drag himself away from the market.

That morning the bullion price surged another $5 to $454 an ounce at the 10.30 a.m. 'fix' in London, for a two-day gain of $55. Gold share prices on the Johannesburg stock exchange were going through the roof.

Buying orders for gold shares flooded into Johannesburg from all over the world. But there was a desperate shortage of stock here too.

The Johannesburg financial institutions, particularly the mining houses, are notorious buyers of gold shares at the bottom of the markets when the investing public are desperate to sell. When the mood changes they invariably become unwilling sellers, causing frantic stock shortages, and squeezing the market higher.

In the recent slide, the institutions had persistently been in the background as reluctant buyers of last resort and brokers with large lines of stock had taken massive discounts just to get rid of them. This morning those same brokers were desperately trying to buy back their shares. But the answer was a very polite, 'No, thank you. We are not selling.'

As Eddie left the trading floor to make the short walk round to Jock McCullough's office, trading was hectic and prices were being bid higher and higher to tempt sellers; as soon as any stock came out it was snapped up.

Eddie still felt the excitement pumping round him as he knocked on McCullough's door.

The chairman, chief executive and major shareholder of Union Mining sat with his feet on his desk, a warm, friendly grin on his face, slowly tapping his knee with an 18-carat-gold letter opener. He watched Eddie walk down the room towards him.

McCullough, a tall, grey-haired 64-year-old with a massive frame still looked every bit the tough, aggressive mine captain he was forty years earlier when he started in the mining industry.

He was one of the old breed of mining men in South Africa who had clawed their way to the top. In McCullough's case it had been from the bottom of a mine. The massive wrinkled hands that had started their working life gripping a pickaxe handle were manicured now. A wafer-thin white gold Piaget glinted from his left wrist. The silk shirt, elegantly tailored trousers and leather shoes from

Lobb's of London were all trappings of success. But in essence, the character of the man had changed very little.

The long legs unfurled themselves from the desk top and McCullough lifted his powerful frame up to its full 6 feet 5 inches. He held out a huge hand.

'Good to see you Eddie.' He pointed to a chair and Eddie sat down. 'I've known your father for years. You look just like him. I thought you should meet some of the people in the investment department. They felt the same way as I did about your gold circular. Horrified.' He grinned at Eddie, and pressed a button on his desk top. A wall panel slid back to reveal a television screen showing the latest gold share prices. They both studied the screen for a moment.

'And looking at the market this morning,' McCullough said with a wicked grin, 'we're the schmucks.' McCullough pressed the button again and the screen disappeared noiselessly.

'Now, you and I must have some lunch.'

'Tell Peter Scofield to come in, and organize some drinks, please,' he rasped to his secretary.

The drinks arrived instantly. They were carried in on silver trays by two black staff wearing white coats and gloves.

The investment team arrived shortly afterwards. Dark suits, white shirts, clean cut, and all out of the same mould. There were four fund managers. They were introduced by McCullough, and, without any prompting, each man gave a brief résumé of his duties for Union Mining. They all ran their own funds, while the combined total assets under their management exceeded R800 million.

More drinks were served on the small roof garden that led from McCullough's office. The views across the skyline of Johannesburg were spectacular on a clear day like today. Once they all had a glass, McCullough said, 'Well, boys, this is the young man who could spoil your batting averages this year.' He smiled at Eddie.

'We're up to our eyes in industrials. If you're right, these boys are wrong. What we want to know Eddie is, have you

37

been lucky in predicting a technical rally in the market, or are you saying we're into a whole new ball game.'

'You read my letter.'

All five men were silent. They had learnt that in the presence of their chairman, they didn't speak unless they were asked.

'America's got a huge deficit and rising inflation, and no one knows how to cure it.' Eddie continued. 'Even if they came up with a miracle cure now it would take at least six months before it had any effect.'

He paused for a moment.

'Investors are going to get panicky when they see share values collapsing. They have to go for gold.'

'So where's gold going?' said McCullough.

'Only one way,' replied Eddie. 'It's trading at $454 this morning. I see it around $800 in the next year to eighteen months.'

'Eight hundred dollars an ounce,' said McCullough. 'Now I know you need your head tested.' He drained his glass. 'Come on gentlemen. It's time I got this madman some lunch.'

'You can't be serious,' said McCullough when they were seated in the intimacy of his small personal dining room. '$800 is a ridiculous price. It will never go that high.'

'You tell me what's going to stop it.'

'Well, I hope to God you know what you're talking about,' said McCullough. 'With all its mining interests this company will be a prime beneficiary. And I take your point about inflation. We bought some new mining equipment last week. The price was up 20 per cent because the manufacturers had to pay more for their raw materials.'

They had cold Cape lobster with a salmon dressing, Tournedos Rossini with fresh asparagus and sauté potatoes. McCullough ordered a dry white Steen with the fish and a red Shiraz with the meat.

Most lobster served in Johannesburg has to be deep frozen because of the city's distance from the sea. This lobster wasn't. It was cooked fresh and Eddie could taste the salt water.

'Flew them in specially for you,' said McCullough. 'Incidentally, I'm sorry about that phone call. We've been having problems with bloody brokers taking us for a ride and your circular caught me on the wrong day.'

A waiter refilled their glasses with Steen and cleared away the lobster plates. Jock McCullough lit a cigarette and inhaled deeply. Eddie caught a glint of the Piaget.

'Eddie, I've got an interesting situation I'd like you to look at. It could make us both some pocket money. I don't know whether your father mentioned it but I own a large farm in Zimbabwe where I'll retire in the next year or so.'

McCullough traced a line across the tablecloth with his finger.

'The main road from Harare to Rochester runs right along the perimeter of the farm. Several times recently my farm manager, Jimmy, has mentioned the increase in traffic. I've got so much on here, I never really gave it a second thought. Jimmy and I were riggers back in the old days together. Three days ago he saw a truck with a drilling rig broken down on the roadside. It had a puncture and the driver was changing the wheel. Jimmy offered to help. When he asked where the rig was going, the driver told him to the old Amanda gold mine – it's about sixty miles into the mountains from my place.'

Eddie knew about the Amanda mine. It was the principal mining asset in a crashed-out penny-stock called Eastern Mining. Eastern Mining was in turn owned by the New-York-based mining house, South African Mining, one of the largest mining conglomerates in South Africa. The mine had not been worked for years.

'Amanda was one of the great old mines,' said McCullough. 'They worked out all the good pay areas years ago, then lost the rich seam that ran through the centre. It's been kept on a care and maintenance basis ever since.

'Eddie, why don't you have a look at it for me. Put your head down in the market. See what you can find out. There are two things you must remember. My name, or this company's name, must never be mentioned. And the first 50,000 shares you buy are mine. Do we have a deal?'

'Yes, Mr McCullough.' For the first time, Eddie allowed himself a broad smile. 'We have a deal.'

9

On his way back from lunch Eddie called in to his office to collect the file on Eastern Mining. Like most investment advisers, Vandermeer & Vandermeer kept a file on every quoted company in the market. It contained press cuttings and sets of accounts for the last five years, as well as the current Extel card on the company's financial statistics.

McCullough was right. As a mining share, Eastern Mining was a dog. It hadn't made a profit for six years, and its mine in Zimbabwe had run out of payable ore. It owned vast tracts of bushland in Zimbabwe and the only reason the shares were standing at eleven cents and not one cent was that every few months someone started a rumour that the land was being sold for grazing. Up went the shares.

There were six million shares in issue; South African Mining held slightly more than 30 per cent. There were no other big holders, leaving about four million floating free.

Eddie checked back copies of the *Rand Morning Mail* for trading volume. There had been no trades in the share that week, but 200,000 shares had changed hands one day the previous week at eleven cents. That was an interesting purchase. The first job was to find out which broker had done the buying. Anyone who bought that many shares in a dud company like Eastern Mining knew something.

He put the file in his briefcase – he would research the fine print later – and left for the market.

As he walked across the trading floor to the Vandermeer desk, he glanced up at the prices board. Gold shares were littered with plus signs though one or two were down from their 'highs' of the day where traders had been tempted to take profits. One of the few gold shares that showed no life at all was Eastern Mining. It stood untraded at eleven cents.

He was greeted by Michael Paisley, a pinstriped, middle-aged Englishman who had been running Vandermeer's trading desk in the stockmarket for the last twelve years.

'Golds are looking good, Eddie. Lot of people talking about the circular.'

'Tell them not to take any notice of it,' he smiled. 'It was written by a madman.' Both men laughed.

'Michael, 200,000 Eastern Mining changed hands last Wednesday. Any idea who did the buying?'

Michael Paisley thought for a while. Very little escaped his eye in the market place, and he normally had the inside track on all the latest market stories.

'I think it was Izzie Van Royen. I had a drink with him at the club bar the other afternoon and he mentioned it. He was buying them for himself. Said he'd heard from a pal of his in Harare there was something going on there. Do you know Izzie?'

Eddie shook his head. 'I know who he is, but I've never met him.'

'He's a bastard. Cute as they come in the market, runs his own show, and doesn't give a damn about anyone. But he's got one hell of a record for picking winners.'

'How do I meet him?'

'Go on the floor and shout for Eastern Mining. You'll meet him all right. When he's operating in a stock he thinks he owns it, so watch your step.'

There were fifteen minutes to go before the 3.30 p.m. close for business. Eddie spotted Izzie Van Royen in one corner of the trading floor and walked towards him. When he started shouting for Eastern Mining, one or two dealers turned their heads but no one approached him with any stock. Most people were writing up their order books before going back to the office, while a few had already started to make their way towards the large gilded doors at the end of the trading floor.

41

'And what for Christ's sake do you think you're doing?' Eddie swung round. It was Van Royen, tall and fiery-eyed.

'Buyer, 200,000 Eastern Mining,' replied Eddie holding his ground.

'Buyer,' bellowed Van Royen. 'You can't be a buyer in this market. I'm a buyer here and I haven't completed my order yet. I'm operating this stock. Who the hell do you think you are?'

'I thought you might be interested in selling me the 200,000 you bought last week.'

Izzie Van Royen looked long and hard at Eddie. Then he said 'I think you and I should have a little chat.'

1 0

Izzie Van Royen was not the sort of man anyone would want to cross at the best of times, but the very last place in the world to confront him was the trading floor of the Johannesburg stock exchange. This for him was the home ground, and here he was at his dangerous best.

Born in the poor Afrikaner suburb of Doornfontein, a derelict district of tenements on the outskirts of Johannesburg, Izzie Van Royen was the youngest of eleven children of one of the poorest families in the area. The Van Royens had lived in Doornfontein as long as any of their neighbours could remember.

Doornfontein had the notable distinction of being one of the few white districts in South Africa to have a sprinkling of black residents. It was so poor and run down that even the stringent South African race laws overlooked it.

With ten brothers and sisters before him, Izzie's parents had little energy or inclination to care for the needs of their youngest son. School was a luxury they could not afford, and like his brothers before him, Izzie did not wear his first pair of shoes until he was twelve years old. Much of his childhood was spent in the shadow of his two elder brothers Johnny and Louis, miners at the local Doornfontein gold mine where their father had worked for forty years before them. They were hulks of men, tall, powerfully built, with straight backs and massive arms. Their bodies had been honed into formidable shape by hours of attacking the rock face with pickaxes in the clammy, sweltering heat of the underground stopes, and they looked at the world with the brazen but simple view of men who are convinced of their physical superiority.

Although still in their early twenties, they had established formidable reputations as face workers on the mine's night shift. Few whites could match their tenacious strength while the Africans called them 'ndoda', which means work-horse.

Izzie hero-worshipped them both. Beneath their brute physicality they were loyal brothers who helped and protected him, but much to Izzie's disappointment, there always seemed to be a point with them at which his age excluded him.

The first time Johnny and Louis took Izzie seriously was when he was seventeen and out on an illicit drinking session with them at Joey's Bar. Like every other bar in Doornfontein, it was a dump; bare boards, sawdust on the floor, the gaudy red and gold décor of the thirties gold-rush days barely visible under the thick layer of brown nicotine covering the walls, ceiling and bar fixtures. A battered radiogram blared out the big band music of the day.

For Izzie it was a dream come true. The three brothers stood in a circle by the bar, slapping each other on the back, and falling about with laughter.

'Hey boys,' shouted Izzie, against the din, 'we'll show 'em who can drink tonight, eh?'

'Nine pints a man,' roared Louis, his big, black-haired barrel chest stretching the seams of his clean, pressed shirt. Tomorrow morning, when the other two complained of hangovers Izzie would stagger around with them. He was at last part of their story.

It started as a small firm pressure in the small of his back from one of the two men standing behind him. Then he felt the hard, bony point of an elbow pushing through. He moved forward a step and half turned.

'Sorry man,' he said in his clipped Afrikaans accent, 'Are you tight for room?'

The man made no reply. He stared insolently at Izzie, his eyes rolling slightly from drunkenness. For a while, Izzie watched him expectantly, waiting for a reply. When there was none, he turned back to his brothers.

'Watch him,' said Louis in Afrikaans. 'He's one of the Ives brothers. They work down the mines with us. They don't like me and Johnny.' Louis glanced over Izzie's shoulder. 'The big, fat guy next to him is his brother.'

'Ever had any trouble with 'em?'

'No, man. Those two wouldn't come near me and Johnny. We'd eat'em alive. But they're English and they're not fond of Afrikaners.'

Then it started again, right in the small of his back.

'One of the Ives brothers keeps pushing me,' said Izzie, his voice flat, the fun and laughter gone.

Both brothers studied him.

'Are you sure?' asked Louis.

Izzie nodded. He could still feel the elbow. Every so often it would push hard into him, then relax.

'What yer gonna do about it, baby brother?' said Johnny, a mischievous twinkle in his eye.

Izzie emptied the remainder of his beer from the bottle and lifted the glass to drink. As he did so a shove from behind propelled him forward and beer spilt down his new shirt and trousers.

'Sorry, man,' said the Ives brother sarcastically. 'I was a bit pushed for room.'

Izzie wiped the beer off his clean, white shirt with one sweep of his hand. It left a dark stain down the front. Slowly Izzie replaced his glass on the bar. His hand coiled round the neck of the empty beer bottle and in one swift movement he picked it up, swung round and smashed it on the Ives brother's skull. The bottle exploded with a pop that silenced the bar and broken fragments of glass crashed through the silence. The Ives brother stood there teetering slightly, his sweaty, red face grinning goonishly. The man remained upright for a few seconds before his legs crumpled beneath him and the heavy body crashed to the sawdust floor. His last impression was the look of murder burning in Izzie's eyes and the hatred etched in the taut, grim lines of his face.

The crowd, always happy to watch a fight, gathered in a circle round Izzie, while the remaining Ives brother swayed at the bar, a half-filled pint of beer in his hand, looking furiously at Izzie. There wasn't a sound. No one moved. All eyes were on young Izzie. He stood alone, moving his bodyweight slowly from one foot to the other, brandishing the jagged neck of the bottle in one hand, the other fist clenched.

'What about you, arse-hole?' Izzie growled at the other Ives brother and spat heavily at his feet.

'You little bastard,' he muttered. And slamming his half-filled beer pot on the bar he lumbered towards Izzie.

He was twice Izzie's size and weight, but Izzie moved swiftly. He side-stepped the first blow, and just as the Ives brother lost balance from the force of it, Izzie slammed the metal toecap of his boot into the soft, plump flesh of his groin. The stab of pain straightened him, and instantly Izzie smacked the broken bottle across the side of his skull. His mouth opened to scream, his eyes bulged with pain, but before a sound could escape, he collapsed at the feet of his already unconscious brother.

Izzie leapt on him, his knees pinning the man's shoulders to the floor. He drew back the broken bottle neck and plunged it forward. Only Johnny's iron grip on his forearm stopped the jagged glass inches from the man's face.

'That's enough, Izzie,' he yelled, tightening the grip on his arm. 'They won't bother us any more. Come on, let's get out of here before the pigs arrive.'

In the peace and safety of another bar on the other side of Doornfontein, Johnny said, 'Jesus, man, you fight like a maniac. That bottle would have killed him.'

Izzie knew it too. He had felt the change in him. Although he lacked the sheer physical strength of his brothers, his speed and animal fury made him a force to be reckoned with. That night at Joey's Bar, Izzie Van Royen came of age.

In the years that followed, very little changed about Izzie Van Royen's basic approach to his adversaries. He no longer cracked them across the skull with a bottle. A long apprenticeship in the stockmarket as first a messenger boy, then a clerk, taught him that the direct approach no longer paid off.

And the battles changed too. No longer was it drunks who wanted to fight, but chairmen who refused to tell.

It didn't take Izzie Van Royen many months of running around the trading floor of the Johannesburg stock exchange to realize the only thing that really mattered was information, good information, information that a man could bet a lifetime's savings on.

Instead of applying his spirit and wits to barroom brawls he now applied them to the long list of gold-mining shares quoted on the Johannesburg stock exchange. He called it doing his 'huiswerk', Afrikaans for homework. Huiswerk was something that had been sadly lacking in Izzie's childhood. But now he had turned it into a long and involved form of research that paid off handsomely. By the time he was thirty-five, Izzie Van Royen had made his first half million and set up as a stockbroker on his own. Five years later he had quadrupled it to two million. After that, the money became less important, but Izzie Van Royen still played the game as keenly as ever.

South Africa produces eighty 80 per cent of the world's gold from the flat, red, dirt gold fields of the Orange Free State and the cluster of mines around the outskirts of Johannesburg itself. Although there are gold share markets in London and New York, the best stories, the real inside information that sends share prices soaring, are most often heard on the trading floor of the Johannesburg stock exchange and the members' bar above it. And this was how the system worked, this was where Izzie Van Royen started his 'huiswerk'.

Over the years Izzie built up, with the help of his

brothers, who had both graduated to mine captains, a network of contacts in the mines around Johannesburg and the Orange Free State that gave him one or several contacts in each mine quoted on the Johannesburg stock exchange's gold board. He built up the network in a variety of ways. No chance was ever missed. He always attended the annual general meeting, even if he had to buy one share to gain entry as a shareholder. He never turned down an opportunity to drink with either of his brothers in the mine bar. He joined the Rand Club, the elite social club, many of whose members are employed in the mining industry around Johannesburg; and in cases where no opportunity presented itself to establish a relationship, he wrote charming letters to the respective mine managers asking if he could visit the mine in his capacity as a stockbroker to write a circular for his clients. He was rarely refused, and more often than not returned the favour, by buying the manager lunch at the Rand Club – and quickly establishing a relationship.

Nor was the service one-way. There were plenty of people on the mines who needed a discreet, one-man-band broker through whom they could make purchases in their own mine's shares at the appropriate time. Izzie Van Royen never betrayed a confidence.

Purchases on price-sensitive information were made in his name through a series of nominee accounts he had with the three major banks in Johannesburg. His reputation in the market and the volume of business he did in gold shares was sufficient to dissuade detailed inquiry by any investigating committee of the Johannesburg stock exchange. Most committee members knew, for they were all stockbrokers too, that to ask Izzie Van Royen why he had bought a share at a particular time was to invite any number of perfectly legitimate answers. Asked once by the president of the exchange why he had bought a large block of Free State Mining a week before the announcement of a massive find of uranium on its Orange Free State lease area, Van Royen replied: 'I liked the look of them on the charts.' To which there is no answer.

While his contacts were perhaps the most important side of Izzie Van Royen's business, there were other aspects he concentrated on. He rarely missed a trick on the trading floor of the stockmarket. Big deals, small deals, put-throughs, you name it. If there was a story behind a purchase or a sale it never took very long to reach Izzie Van Royen's ears. He knew all the head dealers of the largest firms, he knew most of their clients and he had a detailed and intimate knowledge of every gold share quoted on the gold board. Any time that knowledge needed updating, he only had to pick up the phone and speak to one of his contacts.

He spent hours studying annual reports, interim statements, and maps of underground workings in the library of the Chamber of Mines across from the stockmarket, evaluating a mining share's true market worth. Night after night, long after the lights in the office blocks around the stockmarket had been switched off and the offices vacated, Izzie Van Royen sat at his desk in his small, fourth-floor office in Rissik Street reading the fine print in annual reports, working out the latest production costs, or simply scheming his next moves in whichever stock he was 'operating' at the time.

It was on such a night that he had received a long distance call from an old friend of his, Bill McDermot, a small, studious Scotsman who was the assistant librarian at the Chamber of Mines. McDermot was always good for a tip and he loved to make a little easy money on the side.

But ever since McDermot transferred to the Zimbabwe Chamber of Mines in Harare to become chief librarian, Izzie Van Royen had been unable to view his trips to the Chamber of Mines library in the same light.

The call came late one evening as Izzie was packing up to go home.

'Izzie?'

He recognized the voice immediately. 'Hey, Bill, how are you? It's hopeless here. No one gives me the right maps anymore.'

Both men chuckled.

'Izzie, I've got to be quick. I'm going out tonight and didn't want to ring you from the office.'

'I'm listening.'

'Each year up here we update our aerial photos of all the mining areas and keep them on file for reference.'

'I know, I know.'

'Today, I was filing the new photos of the old Amanda mine. Izzie, they're very different from last year. Then the mine was barren. Now there are all sorts of new buildings. We have no records of new permissions being granted, but it's an existing mine, so they wouldn't necessarily need them.'

'I don't suppose . . .'

McDermot laughed. 'Copies are in the post today, registered mail. Amanda's been a dead duck for years but you never know. . . . If you start buying, count me in.'

When Izzie hung up, he went to his filing cabinet and pulled out the file on Amanda Mining. He flicked through the chairman's statement in the latest set of accounts and ringed a paragraph.

It read: 'During the next few months we shall test drill the outer lease of the Amanda mine before dismantling the mine buildings for scrap. The area has been drilled in the past and it is not expected any new area worth mining will be found.' The statement was signed 'Mark Ashford, chairman.'

He dropped the accounts into his briefcase for further study later. He had watched with interest the growth of Mark Ashford's mining empire. Now it was time to do a little 'huiswerk'.

I I

Eddie stepped out of the elevator on the fourth floor and followed the sign round the corridor to the offices of I. Van Royen, Stockbroker. The door was open so he walked in.

'I'm in here,' called Van Royen. 'Follow your nose and you'll reach me.'

Van Royen's office was sparsely furnished with solid, army-surplus-type furniture. The walls were bare and painted a dull cream. The woodwork was dark and brown and covered in dust. There were no curtains on the metal windows and the carpets were loose fitting and threadbare. Had he not known better, Eddie would have thought Izzie Van Royen was going out of business.

'Sit yourself down, boy,' said Van Royen, walking across to a battered old fridge in one corner of the office. 'What will you have? There's beer or scotch,' he asked.

'Beer, please.'

The older man pulled two cold pint cans from the fridge and handed one to Eddie. There were no glasses. Both men ripped open the tops and drank from the cans.

'Now then,' said Van Royen, slowly moving back to his desk. 'I have two questions for you. Who told you I bought those 200,000 Eastern Mining? And what business is it of yours if I did?' He took a long draught of beer and belched loudly.

There was no point in concealing information. An operator like Van Royen would never move into a share like Eastern Mining unless he knew something.

'I've got a client who thinks they might open up the old Amanda mine. The road up to the mine passes alongside his farm and he's noticed the increased traffic.'

Not a flicker of surprise showed on Van Royen's face. 'What do you mean "might" open the Amanda. They *have* opened up the bloody Amanda.' Van Royen strode out of the room and came back with a thin blue cardboard file. 'Now, I want your word you'll get lockjaw about these.'

Eddie nodded and pulled his chair nearer the desk. 'You've got it.'

Van Royen picked a photograph from the file and laid it on the desk.

'This is an aerial photograph of Amanda twelve months ago taken by the Zimbabwe Chamber of Mines on a routine survey of the area.'

He placed another newer, brighter looking photograph beside it. 'This is an aerial photograph of Amanda taken two weeks ago.'

Eddie scrutinized both photos. The old mine area showed up clear and white on both photos. But there was a dark rectangle running down the side of the mine in the latest photograph. He looked closer.

'Here, use that,' said Van Royen, sliding a large, round, hand magnifying glass across the desk. Eddie focused it on the darkened area.

'It's a new accommodation block for black mine workers,' said Van Royen.

'But there's been no announcement,' said Eddie. 'I checked back through the company statements and press cuttings.'

'It so happens . . .' Van Royen smiled mischievously, 'that Eastern Mining has its annual general meeting soon. I think maybe we'll hear something then.'

'Come with me.' Van Royen led Eddie into the next office. He unlocked a heavy metal door, and both men stepped into a large room-safe with shelves from floor to ceiling, crammed with box files, papers and rolled maps.

Van Royen pointed at the shelves. 'Mining shares aren't about cash flows and balance sheets as you youngsters are taught. They're about maps, documents, photographs. You know,' he said, 'I've got maps of old mines here the boys down at the Chamber of Mines would give their right arms for.'

He lifted a stack of papers and rolled maps off one of the shelves and handed them to Eddie. 'Put those on my desk. I'll bring some more.'

For almost an hour they pored over maps of the Amanda gold mine and drank more beer. Eddie was amazed at the amount of information Van Royen had accumulated. There were detailed drawings of old workings, coloured plans of the mine's now exhausted ore reserves, and a large plan of the main pay shoots of gold bearing reef.

'Look at this one here,' said Van Royen, his finger tracing the line of the mine's gold-bearing reef. 'It faults just here and that's the end of it. If they've picked that up further on down the lease area, Amanda will have a bonanza. That reef had some of the highest grade ore in Southern Africa. At today's prices, the profits would be fabulous.'

Eddie was totally absorbed. It looked like Jock McCullough was right. And the photographs of the new building were proof.

Finally, Izzie Van Royen said, 'I'm flying up to Zimbabwe tomorrow night to have a closer look at Amanda. A pal of mine is lending me his old jeep. Why don't you come along? We'll be back in Johannesburg by Sunday.'

12

Harare, Zimbabwe
Saturday 17 September
4.30 p.m.

The jeep roared through the heavy heat of the later afternoon as it sped across the dry Zimbabwean bush leaving behind a trail cloud of swirling red dust.

Izzie Van Royen reached down to the ice cooler between his feet and pulled out two bottles of cold beer. He snapped the tops off against the metal ridge on the door of the jeep and handed one to Eddie, who was driving.

'If we don't find this mine before dark, we're done for Eddie,' he said. 'We haven't got any gear to sleep out in and it's a six-hour drive back to Harare.'

The sun sat right on top of a range of hills in front of him. The sky was blazing pink and shadows across the bush were lengthening.

'We've got about an hour,' said Eddie. 'We'll find it.'

He pushed the jeep into third gear and stepped on the accelerator. They careered off, bucking and bumping down the badly pot-holed dirt road, the crate of beer bottles in the ice bucket clinking above the roar of the engine.

'Thank Christ for the beer, man,' yelled Izzie, finishing his sixth bottle. 'This would be bloody murder if I wasn't half pissed.'

A pair of black Desert Hawks circled lazily through the late afternoon thermals over a clump of trees, their sharp eyes ever watchful for movement on the ground.

The flat bushland road stretched out to a range of hills, but there was no sign of the mine. Eddie stared resolutely ahead at the ball of shimmering heat further down the road, watching the eddying patterns changing.

A white post flicked into focus. He frowned and squinted hard. There it was again. He changed down, accelerated and pulled back to fourth gear at maximum revs.

'There's a sign ahead,' said Eddie pointing down the road. He could see it quite clearly now.

Izzie shielded the fading sunlight from his eyes with his left hand.

'I've got you,' he shouted. 'Amanda Gold Mine – sixteen kilometres,' he read aloud slowly as they drew nearer.

They swung off the bush road onto a single track leading up into the mountains. Dusk edged closer all the time.

'Let her have it,' said Izzie banging the door panel with the palm of his hand. 'Now we'll see what these bastards have been up to.'

They climbed up into the mountains, the stillness of the early evening only broken by the roar of the jeep's engine as it fought its way up the steep, twisting road.

'There's another sign down there,' yelled Izzie as the jeep came up over the top of the ridge and descended into a flat open pass, bordered either side by mountains. They drove on for a few minutes and pulled up at the sign.

'Amanda Gold Mine – General Office,' it said. An arrow pointed off the road to the mine entrance, two tall black metal gates with strands of barbed wire running across the top.

Any further view of the mine was obstructed by the general office, a wide timbered building several yards long behind the gates, and a huge wall of sand. This was part of a massive semi-circular 'slimes dam' built around the front section of the old mine by the early miners.

Slimes dams look like huge deposits of natural sand. They are built of the sandy waste material left after rock from the mine face has been broken down by a crusher and put through the gold extraction process.

The gates were padlocked and there was no sign of life.

'Drive down the road a while and we'll find a spot to get over those slimes,' said Izzie.

They stretched in a solid wall for a mile along the bush road.

'Pull over here, boy,' said Izzie eventually, pointing to some trees just ahead. 'No one will see us in this light.'

They climbed through the barbed-wire fence and clawed their way up the massive sandy bank.

Izzie was first to reach the top, where a large white sign proclaimed 'Private Property. Trespassers Will Be Prosecuted.'

They crouched behind the rim of the slimes dam gazing down at the mine compound in silent amazement. It was a full ten seconds before either of them spoke.

Immediately below them, picked out in the arc lights of the compound, were two gleaming new mine shafts, complete with headgear for lifting men, machines, and rock. Behind the shafts, on the perimeter of the compound, was a line of new buildings. Three of them were completed, while the fourth had a frame of iron girders where there should have been a roof.

Two larger buildings were at the other end of the mine. One was a new refinery with round, elevated washtanks and a tall chimney. Next to it, and still under construction, was a smelter. A fleet of ore-carrying trucks were parked to one side of the old crushing plants, where the rock is broken down and transported to the refinery. A network of roads, recently graded, spread out into the middle distance.

'I don't believe it,' said Izzie. 'This isn't exploratory drilling. The bastards are building a brand new mine without saying a word to anyone.'

Izzie took his binoculars from his coat pocket and focused on the general office. Lights had been switched on and he could see someone moving around quite plainly. He checked the rest of the mine but it appeared deserted.

'Somehow we've got to get into that office and have a look at their maps. If there's only one coon down there we'll be all right. If there's a gang of them we'll be in trouble. Saturday evening – they'll be getting juiced out of their skulls.'

They slid back down the side of the slimes dam, reversed the jeep and drove back to the main entrance. This time Izzie was in the driving seat. As he approached the mine gates, he switched the headlights on full beam, and with a clenched fist, stabbed out three long blasts on the horn.

The jeep roared to a halt in a cloud of dust. No one appeared, so he gave two more blasts on the horn. A moment later, the office door opened and a black security guard ambled down the general office steps and across the compound towards them.

'Come on man! Open up. Open up. We haven't got all day while you sit on your butt,' shouted Izzie.

The guard broke into a trot. Without a word he unlocked the main gates and pulled one side back so the jeep could drive into the compound.

Izzie drew up in front of the main office, switched off the engine and jumped out.

'Booysens, mining engineer, Eastern Mining, Johannesburg,' he said. 'Head office sent us here.'

'Pass?' inquired the guard with a shy grin.

Izzie's cold grey eyes bore down on him. 'Pass!' he snapped back. 'Don't you start getting smart with me, kaffir.'

The guard was visibly confused. His orders from the mine manager were to let no one into the mine without a pass, yet this Afrikaner was an even more important boss from Johannesburg. He had heard of the city, but he had never been there.

Izzie caught sight of the radio aerial on the roof of the office and gambled there would be no one at the other end on a Saturday night. He looked contemptuously at the guard.

'Don't just stand there, you bloody monkey. Get on the radio and ask someone who does know.' He turned to Eddie. 'Come on, boy, we've got work to do.'

They strode up the steps into the main office and went straight to a side office marked 'Manager'. Behind them they could hear the guard repeating his call sign to Harare.

'Quick,' said Eddie, pointing to the maps and charts around the walls. 'Check this lot for grades and borehole results. We've got about sixty seconds.'

They worked on opposite sides of the room – each scanning the mass of multi-coloured maps and sections of the Amanda gold mine.

'Over here,' Izzie said suddenly. He stood riveted to a large blue and red map on the wall. 'Boreholes.' He swept his finger in a line across the map. 'And right down the line of the main seam, six new shafts. But Christ, Eddie, look at these recovery grades. Fourteen grams a ton, fifteen, twelve, sixteen . . . these are some of the richest gold values I've ever seen.'

'And look at these claims they've pegged,' said Eddie, pointing to a map next to the borehole results. Blocks of claims extending to six square miles had been coloured green, surrounding Amanda's existing mining ground which was painted in red. The green claims were four times larger than the red.

Another map showed a network of recently constructed roads going out into the lease areas and the level to which they were to be graded.

'Do we dare take any of these?' Eddie looked around the room. There was a photocopier on top of an old map chest. 'They're making this too easy.' He grinned at Izzie.

The first few copies the machine spewed out were faint but then they grew darker. They took two of the best copies, switched off the machine and pinned the map back on the wall.

'No evidence,' said Eddie, folding the faint copies, and tucking them inside his shirt.

56

'Let's get out of here,' said Izzie, having a last glance at the maps.

As soon as he heard them walk into the main office, the guard put down his radio receiver.

'No luck?' Izzie asked him stony-faced.

'No luck, sar.'

'Where are the rest of the boys?'

The guard pointed out of the window to the mountains beyond. 'With their wives. There is just me.'

A broad smile spread across Izzie's face. He looked straight into the guard's eyes and put a warm, friendly hand on his shoulder.

'You know,' he beamed, 'I told you a terrible lie.'

'Lie, sar?'

'We don't work for Eastern Mining, but we are shareholders in the company – so we have a right to know what's going on.'

The guard stepped back. He did not understand. His right hand gripped the long, wooden truncheon that hung from a clip on the side of his belt. No more did he trust this Afrikaner he thought was a boss. He only knew his orders. No one was to enter this compound. 'You must go now or we fight,' he said.

Izzie pulled out his wallet and flipped it open. He counted out five twenty-rand bills. He knew it was more than the guard would earn in a month. 'If you tell the boss we have been here they will fire you immediately. There will be no more beer and no more food for your children. Forget you ever saw us, and this money is for you.'

Izzie dropped the money on the table.

'Remember,' cautioned Izzie, 'if you say anything, they'll kick you out.'

'Not say, boss. Not say,' whispered the guard excitedly as he counted the notes. Then he tucked them away in his shirt pocket. 'What can I tell? There has been nothing.'

'That's my boy,' said Izzie, giving him a hearty slap across the shoulder.

'C'mon Eddie. We've got a long drive ahead of us.'

They drove out of the compound into the darkness. Izzie

snapped the tops off two more beer bottles. 'Eddie, we're going to make a pile,' he yelled above the noise of the engine. 'Those bastards have got a brand new mine sitting there in a bombed-out, ten-cent stock, and no one knows about it except them and us.'

They drank beer all the way home, laughing like hyenas in the bush night, as the jeep careered back through the bush to Harare and civilization.

13

Johannesburg
Monday 19 September
9.30 a.m.

Eddie was one of the first few brokers at his desk when the Johannesburg stock exchange opened for business the following Monday morning. For an institution that transacts a large part of the world's gold share business, either directly or through the New York and London markets, the Johannesburg stock market has an uncanny resemblance to a church hall.

At one end are the ornate wooden entrance doors, while the trading floor is long and narrow and planked in wood with a high nave-like roof above it. A prices board carrying the latest quotations runs the length of the exchange and a platform at its base enables the African 'boys' to change prices as demand dictates. Across the other side of the trading floor, facing the prices board, are tiers of desks for the dealers. Eddie stood at his, in a line of many, watching the other brokers filing into the exchange.

He had arrived back from Harare late the previous evening and crept into bed beside Lucy. She seemed to be in such a deep sleep, he didn't have the heart to wake her. He spent a restless night, drowsing intermittently. Each time he woke, he calculated the profits to be made. He used various permutations with a different number of shares and a higher or lower share price, but every time the final figures had the same common denominator. The profits were enormous. This time he was going to be very rich. Very quickly. All he had to do was to buy in a sizeable amount of shares and wait for the announcement.

He woke for the last time at daybreak, and moved quietly through the shower, dressing, breakfast routine so as not to wake the rest of the family. He arrived at his office at seven o'clock just as the cleaners were leaving.

For two hours he pored over the past five years of accounts from Eastern Mining and read every press cutting in the firm's files on the company. There was no mention of any new mine. The only reference to the area was in the chairman's statement for the year ending 30 September 1976, when he said that a 'prospecting operation was being undertaken on various southern Zimbabwe lease areas but these are not expected to yield any exceptional prospects about which the company and its shareholders do not already have full knowledge'.

By the time Eddie had unlocked the Vandermeer & Vandermeer market desk and sorted through the day's buying and selling orders, a steady stream of dealers had filled the trading floor and the first few deals of the day were being transacted.

He and Izzie had already worked out a dealing scheme and he had telephoned McCullough and told him of the find.

'Just what I thought,' said McCullough. 'Don't forget, you buy my shares first.'

Once his own dealing staff had been organized for the day, Eddie stepped down into the hubbub of the trading floor to implement the dealing plan. The scheme had a double objective.

The first stage was to buy a significant number of shares without moving the price too much. The second was to move the share price substantially by sparking speculation about the new mine. This would alert Eastern Mining's board that the market suspected a strike and expected a statement.

If they hadn't planned a statement at the forthcoming annual general meeting, they would be forced to make one now. And the shares would rocket. He glanced up at the gold board. Eastern Mining were offered at nine cents.

He yelled the name of the stock two or three times and then a cheery voice behind him said, 'That's me, Eddie.' It was Doug Anderson. They had been at school together in Natal, and had partnered each other in the school tennis team. Eddie was glad to be dealing with a friend.

'How big is the market, Doug?'

'As big as you want. I've got an institution that's clearing out a parcel of stock they've had since the days when Eastern Mining made profits. There's 200,000 on offer at nine cents and probably the same again a little higher.'

'I'll take the 200,000 at nine. Will you ask about the rest?'

'Sure thing. Why the hell are you buying this crap? Eastern Mining hasn't made a profit for years.'

'Some of the boys want to have a punt. They've heard some story or other. You know what it's like. If you get the other 200,000 I'll keep you covered for 10,000 for a day or two.'

Anderson nodded agreement and left the trading floor at a brisk trot to ring his client.

Eddie picked up another 100,000 shares in odd lots at nine cents and made the price on the board ten-cent bid. The 'B' beside the price meant there was an active bidder in the market. Doug Anderson delivered the extra 200,000 shares at ten cents and Eddie tempted another 50,000 shares into the market by making Eastern Mining eleven-cents bid. But there were no sellers after that.

He glanced at his watch. It was after 9.45 a.m. In fifteen minutes he had cleaned the market out of 550,000 shares. Both men agreed to share the opening purchases equally, which after Jock McCullough's 50,000 and 10,000 shares Eddie had undertaken to hold for Doug Anderson, left them with 245,000 each. On an issued share capital of six million shares, they owned about 8 per cent of Eastern Mining and the new Amanda mine.

That was sufficient for now. He walked back to the dealing desk and looked around the market to see if his activities had aroused any interest. No one appeared to be watching him. He glanced over at Izzie Van Royen's desk. Izzie was sitting back in his chair, his feet on his desk, smoking a cigarette and blowing smoke rings aimlessly. No one looked less interested in the activities on the trading floor. Eddie dialled his number.

'We've both got 245,000 each and I'm holding 10,000 for Doug Anderson for a couple of days.'

'Good boy. Now we'll give her a go.'

Izzie stubbed out his cigarette and swung into action. He skipped lightly down the steps from his desk on to the trading floor. He was grim-faced, alert, and fiery-eyed. When it came to horse-trading on the market floor, Izzie Van Royen was a holy terror. He had stitched up so many young dealers that most firms would only allow their senior dealing staff to do business with him.

Striding towards the centre of the trading floor he started shouting.

'Eastern Mining . . . Eastern Mining. Come on now you bastards, give me yer stock. Twelve cents, thirteen cents, fourteen cents. This stock's going to the moon.' His raucous, heavily accented, Afrikaans voice cut through the general babble. Heads turned and a dealer stepped forward, his dealing book raised to do business. Immediately their heads went together.

'Come on you bastards. Fourteen cents I'm paying for this shit. Eastern Mining fourteen cents. The stock's going to the moon.'

A crowd gathered around him. He bought 60,000 shares at fourteen cents and then bid the price up to nineteen cents.

'Come on, let's have the rest of it,' he yelled at the group around him. 'I'm not going to steal it from you like a council member of the Johannesburg stock exchange – I'm going to pay you nineteen cents a share.'

The crowd fell about laughing. Izzie Van Royen had a deep-seated belief that the biggest crooks and thieves in

61

the Johannesburg stock exchange sat on the twelve-man council of senior brokers who ran it. He never lost an opportunity to say so and on the trading floor of the JSE it always got a great reception.

'Nineteen cents bid. That's what I'll pay for this shit, and I'll buy any amount you like.' It was the usual Van Royen performance – he danced around the floor, arms flying in all directions, yelling obscenities about the stock-exchange committee. He was even worse when he had been drinking at lunch-time. Then it was the best matinée show in town. He managed to pick up three more parcels of shares before going back to his desk.

Izzie Van Royen's record for spotting cheap stocks where something was just about to happen was legendary in the market. Before he had even left the trading floor two other brokers were bidding for Eastern Mining and by the time he got back to his desk and surveyed the scene, Eastern Mining had moved up to twenty-one cents bid. A handful of dealers were clamouring for the stock now. Izzie picked up the phone and dialled.

'Is that the *Exchange Telegraph* news desk?'

'Yes.'

'I've got a story for your market report. Eastern Mining has gone from nine cents to twenty-one cents bid this morning. They say they've discovered a new mine or something.'

'Thanks for the tip, we'll have a look at it.'

Fifteen minutes later Izzie stood over the *Exchange Telegraph* ticker tape smiling to himself. He read: 'Eastern Mining have risen sharply throughout the morning on heavy turnover amidst rumours that the company will soon be announcing details of a new mining venture.'

The story, transmitted to every brokers' office, bank and newsroom in the country, generated its own speculative following, and by 11 a.m. Eastern Mining had pushed to twenty-six cents.

As soon as Izzie had left the trading floor, it was part of the plan that Eddie should step in and do some more buying just in case the other fish didn't bite. He snapped up odd lot parcels of shares at twenty cents and another 50,000 at twenty-one cents. He sat at the firm's desk in the market feeding figures into the desk calculator. He and Izzie now owned 600,000 shares, exactly 10 per cent of Eastern Mining at an average price of sixteen cents a share. And that was without Izzie's latest purchases.

He glanced up at the prices board. Eastern Mining were trading at twenty-eight cents. After brokerage expenses, the pair of them had a profit of ten cents a share on 600,000 shares, or in straight cash terms R60,000. That was a profit of R30,000 each in a little over two hours. Not bad, Eddie mused as he watched the figures flash up on the screen of the calculator. But the fun was only just beginning.

14

London
Monday 19 September
5.00 p.m.

Standing at the window of the penthouse office overlooking the Thames, Mark Ashford, the tall, suave chairman of South African Mining sipped a large 25-year-old Glenfiddich on the rocks from a heavy cut-glass tumbler.

He was not a private drinker by habit, but on this occasion he could not share the celebration with any other member of staff on the eight floors of South African Mining offices below him.

He lifted the glass and sucked a mouthful of whisky through the ice. 'A small, private celebration,' he said to himself, toasting the cold, grey Thames as it slid silently by below him in the fading autumn light.

He was a handsome man, elegantly dressed in black silk suit, white shirt and black and white polka-dot silk tie. Although he followed the sombre grey and black dress code of the London banking world, he conformed his own way. The cut and style of his clothes was distinctly slick.

Half an hour earlier, he had bought all the mineral lease areas around the Amanda. If the rich new vein of ore on the Amanda continued outside its current mineral lease area, Mark Ashford owned it. In just a few days, he thought, sipping at his drink, 'I'll have the whole bloody lot.'

His plan was a simple one and exhibited Mark Ashford's flair for fraud. He had set up the deal as he had many times before through his old friends at the Union Bank of Switzerland, and, as always, carefully wrapped it in a cloak of official secrecy. The bank was signing the purchase as nominees while the Swiss banking laws on financial disclosure would ensure total secrecy.

Once he owned Amanda, he would give the two directors he was dining with that night a 5 per cent interest each, to ensure full cooperation and their signatures to the various schemes he had evolved for losing the £1.5 million of South African Mining's money he had spent already developing the Amanda. In return, both men would sign an agreement only to sell their shares back to him. Each man would buy his 5 per cent for £200,000. Neither had this kind of money, so Mark Ashford arranged loans for them through the Union Bank. He would borrow the money from the bank, then re-lend it. Their loan agreements would contain clauses that the loan was repayable within seven days on demand.

Mark Ashford used each man's 5 per cent interest as collateral for the loan. The net effect of all this was that while both men technically owned their shares, control of them lay with Ashford. So long as they kept on the right side of him, the loans would never be called and they could enjoy the substantial dividend payments that would soon start to flow.

That was how Mark Ashford liked to operate. He never went into a situation he did not ultimately control. He never did business with a man he didn't control either. And if he couldn't play the ball, then he went for the man. Before he embarked on any major deal with anyone, he spent a good deal of time and money building up a private

64

file on them. If, for any reason, the play ever got away from him, Mark Ashford always knew he could fell the man with the ball.

Should the bank be asked, it bought the lease on behalf of three investor clients from Zurich with a small ranching company in southern Zimbabwe who wanted the land for cattle grazing. Perfectly plausible. The cattle-rearing business in Zimbabwe was good business to be in and it made financial sense to expand it.

Below him the lines of evening traffic clogged the Embankment and the stream of people hurrying to the tube station flattened out to cover the pavement as more and more people poured out onto the street from the long line of offices either side of the South African Mining London office.

He gazed across at the cold, grey Thames and mapped out his evening. A drink in the office, a steam bath and massage at the Mayfair Japanese baths and then on to dinner at the Savoy with his two closest directors. He would break the news of the Amanda lease to them over a magnum of Krug and then go home. Which one would he have waiting? He flicked through the faces and bodies he had hired before.

Mark Ashford never had girlfriends. He used to call them his girlfriends, but an unusual feature of his many relationships was that he never put himself in a situation that demanded any emotional pull or involvement. And over the years it had become apparent to him that for real sexual gratification he needed to pay. Hard cash got him off.

His current 'girlfriend', a young lady called Alicia, was ideally suited. She was twenty-two, twenty years younger than Mark, long blonde hair, a centrefold body, and there was nothing she wouldn't do for money. Fast cars, expensive clothes, trips abroad and big houses. This was the life she longed for.

Mark Ashford saw the whole story and loved it. His delight came from watching her response when he passed over the money. Most of his working days ended, propped up by two pillows, naked in bed, slowly counting out ten-pound notes as she slavishly attended his needs. Each time she heard the rustle of another crisp ten-pound note from the wad in his left hand, she worked harder.

The soft buzz of the phone broke his thoughts.

'Max Llewellyn from Johannesburg,' said his secretary.

'Mark?' asked the calm, measured voice of the senior partner of Llewellyn & Partners, the largest broking firm on the Johannesburg stock exchange.

'Hello Max. Good to hear from you,' said Mark Ashford in expansive mood. 'What's new?'

'The story is you've had a big find at the Amanda. A couple of the boys here have been buying big blocks of Eastern Mining and moved the price up from nine cents to twenty-nine cents.'

'What?' yelled Mark Ashford.

'Is there anything in it? Perhaps you should issue a statement?'

There was silence. Mark Ashford thought fast. Who could possibly know? He had taken every precaution.

'Who are the buyers?'

'Two local brokers, Izzie Van Royen and Eddie Vandermeer. Don't know much about Vandermeer, he's been in London for three years, but we all know Van Royen. The guy's an eccentric, got his own small broking firm and is one of the roughest traders in the market. He's got a hell of a reputation for picking winners – when he moves, he pumps a lot of money into a stock and he's nearly always on the inside track. Just looking at the volume of business done today, something like thirteen per cent of Eastern Mining's shares have changed hands. The pair of them could have picked up ten per cent of the company.'

'OK Max, leave it to me overnight and I'll talk to my people in Johannesburg. I'm sure I would have been told if there's any truth in it. I'll come back to you before the market opens in the morning. We may want to off-load some stock.'

Ashford replaced the phone, consumed by a mixture of

fear and fury. He was in serious danger of being exposed as little more than a common liar and thief.

He had known for months about the massive new deposit of gold his mining engineer had found at Amanda, and for over a year he had been using cash from his master company, South African Mining, to develop it. Not a word had he said to shareholders, for this was the break he had been waiting for. For years, he had watched the hard-earned profits of his toil being distributed to shareholders in the form of dividend payments on South African Mining shares. This was the deal that was going to set him apart from the vast herd of financiers who make a million or so but never hit the really big money. This was the deal that was going to put Mark Ashford right at the top of the international financial stack, and no one was going to take it away from him. Of that he was absolutely certain.

Mark Ashford's interest in money started at an early age. He was nine and still at school, where his weakest subject was maths. An intelligent boy in every other respect, Mark Ashford's intellect had one sensitive flaw. He could add and subtract with ease, but he just could not understand fractions and decimals. He had a block. In maths class, when he had to stand up and work out sums publicly, his mind went blank and he was seized with terror. His classmates laughed at him and some of his answers to more difficult questions had them rocking in their desks.

It started to undermine his natural confidence. For forty minutes twice a week he was an object of derision for his maths teacher and the subject of ridicule by his classmates – most of whom he could better in every other subject and sport.

It was a problem. Even his grandma made references to it on his weekly trip to her flat for lunch and pocket money. For Grandma to even acknowledge he had a failing was a serious warning, for Grandma Ashford had her own particular weakness – the blind adoration of her only grandson, her darling 'Markey'. The heir apparent to her only son and the standard-bearer of the Ashford bloodline, little Mark was the embodiment of a lifetime's dreams for Grandma Ashford.

She was a warm, broad, big-hearted woman – not an obvious beauty, for at sixty-eight her good looks had disappeared with age. But she was tall and always immaculately turned out. Her lightly tinted grey hair was perfectly set as it had been for the last fifteen years by the same hairdresser in Golders Green. The matching pastel skirts and blouses, classically cut in the finest cottons and silks, always looked chic, and her sleek handmade Italian shoes were brightly polished and never scratched.

Her hands were beautifully manicured, the perfectly rounded nails painted deep shades of red, and around her wrist a selection of heavy gold chains clinked and jangled.

The highlight of Grandma's week was the one weekly visit she received from her grandson. It was the only time she had him completely to herself. Over the years she had noted the little boy's favourite treats, and she made this weekly lunch an hour-long session of indulgence. Whatever he wanted he got. He only had to ask.

Something happened on one of these visits that was to stamp an indelible trait on his fast-developing character and to colour his early view of how to achieve dreams and overcome problems. It was an incident that gave Mark Ashford a devastating insight into human weakness, and turned out to be one that he used with ruthless cunning throughout his life.

It was November, damp and cold, and Mark had left the rest of his classmates bracing themselves for a game of rugby. It hadn't taken many afternoons of charging up and down the rugby pitch in freezing conditions for him to realize that this was not how he wished to spend his time. A cry of agony in a muddy, loose scrum, a vicious limp, and Mark was excused games for the rest of the season.

He arrived at Grandma Ashford's flat shortly after two o'clock for his Wednesday lunch, a week after his ninth birthday. From the moment he stepped through the front door onto the thick, bouncy hall carpet and into the soft warm embrace of Grandma, Mark felt an immediate sense of relief and wellbeing. He was back in the promised land, the place of plenty.

She quickly sat him down in the chair, propped him up with cushions, and put a tray on his lap. Lunch at Grandma's was always the same. A glass of orange juice, hot salt beef sandwiches, a chocolate biscuit – Penguins were his favourite – and a large chunk of Turkish delight, heavily dusted with icing sugar.

'I must talk to you my darling. I have been talking with your mother and we are worried about these sums of yours.' She paused and turned a diamond ring on her finger. 'How are the sums, Markey?'

Mark pretended not to hear, and set about his lunch enthusiastically. Why did she always have to ask?

'Not too bad, Grandma. I think I've got 'em a bit better now.'

'Markey,' she continued, 'I have been talking to your mother. We have found the answer. When I have finished with you, Markey, you will be an Einstein.' She clapped her hands and her bracelets rattled. 'I have found the answer for you, Markey,' she said with great pride.

Mark sat and listened intently to his grandmother. He was immediately interested. How could Grandma help his maths? She leant across the table and clasped his hands in hers. 'Markey,' she said in an excited whisper, 'I will teach you how to do the sums, and you will help Grandma with her banking.'

Little Mark watched her closely. Grandma's banking had immediate appeal. Any favour for Grandma met instant reward. Even in Mark's short life he had learnt banking meant money.

'How?' he asked.

'My darling, you know my eyes are not so good. I have trouble all the time to see the figures. I do not like to ask your father – he is much too busy – and they are very nice about it at the bank, but they are always busy too. I need you to help with my figures. In return, darling, I will help you with your sums.'

Mark did not see how helping Grandma add up her weekly expenses would help him understand fractions and decimals, but he knew his grandma always acted in his best interest, and he readily agreed.

'All right, Grandma. When do we start?'

'Straight away,' she said. She pulled out her cheque book from her handbag, and slid it across to Mark.

'Each week you will fill the numbers in for Grandma down here,' she told him, pointing at the tally stub. 'Then you will write the cheque. I will sign it, and you will collect the money from the bank. I have arranged everything.'

'Each week £200 comes into my account from your grandfather's trust. Every time you cash a cheque we take the amount from the £200. You will always be able to tell me how I'm getting along. You will be my accountant, my man of figures.'

As with other children, Mark was at an age where he was rapidly appreciating the pleasures money could buy and the highlight of his afternoon teas with Grandma was the collection of his two-pounds-a-week pocket money. 'Markey, my darling, your Grandmama is getting old. It is difficult for me to walk to the bank. I cannot see the figures to do my accounts. I cannot write the letters, I cannot even read my book anymore. I don't mind Markey, I don't mind. For me it is not so important. I have a telephone, everyone comes to see me, we talk and laugh and make coffee, I don't mind. The doctor says he can do nothing without the hospital and the operation on the eyes, but I don't want that Markey, I am too old.'

She paused to unwrap his Penguin.

'Now then,' she said, reaching for her bag again. 'Where is your pocket money?'

Mark's eyes widened greedily at the click of the buckle as Grandma opened the bag. She pulled out a long crocodile-skin wallet. She flicked the wallet open and offered it to her young grandson. 'Take your pocket money for me Markey,' she said. He hesitated for a moment, then leant forward, and with both hands, took the wallet from her. There they were, three thick lines of crisp, new, coloured notes, tucked into the tight compartments. He caught the scent of their newness, it was a smell he was never to forget. He ran his fingers over the notes.

'Don't be so shy, my darling, you must take your two pounds for Grandma.'

In a flash of inspiration, Mark realized he could take more than two pounds, much more. Grandma wouldn't challenge him. If she missed the money she wouldn't be sure, with her failing sight that the mistake wasn't hers. It seemed safe enough.

He took a new five-pound note, laid it on his lap and quickly plucked out a one-pound note. He put the one on top of the five, folded them, and held them up for inspection. 'Thanks, Grandma,' he grinned across the table and tucked the notes into his inside jacket pocket. Then he handed her back the wallet and moved round the table to give her the customary kiss.

Minutes later he was on his way home, his heart pounding from the excitement of having stolen money.

The following week at lunch with Grandma, he repeated the same sleight of hand while taking his pocket money. Nothing had been said about the previous week's theft and Grandma's wallet was still bulging with crisp new notes.

Mark also took up his new role as Grandma's cashier for the first time. He went to the bank after lunch, and collected the money.

During the following months, his performance in maths improved dramatically. His homework was among the best in the class, his confidence improved, and his teacher viewed him with new respect.

Mark's thefts from Grandma also became more sophisticated as finally her eyesight failed completely, and all she could do was sign her cheques where he held her hand. Not once did Grandma ever miss the money. Every two or three weeks, when a surplus had built up in her current account, Mark changed the one hundred pounds he withdrew for her each week to two hundred, putting the spare hundred pounds in a secret place beneath the floorboards of his attic playroom.

She died a year later, aged sixty-nine, and her estate was parcelled up and distributed among the family. Surprisingly, Grandma Ashford had not been quite so well off as her family had thought and most members of the family were privately amazed at how little money the old lady had left. Everyone, that is, except Mark. For in the eighteen months he had been the old lady's bookkeeper, he had managed by various means to transfer a respectable proportion of her cash from the safety of her current account to his playroom floor. When she died he had tucked away the princely sum of £4367.00.

Thirty years later, Mark Ashford was still stealing, but the sleight of hand with Grandma's wallet had blossomed into sophisticated financial theft from the investing public who bought mining shares on the stockmarkets of London, New York and Johannesburg.

It started with the help of a London merchant bank who found him a small listed company with a little cash and some mining assets on the rich Orange Free State gold mines, sixty miles outside Johannesburg.

There was a new discovery of ore, the share price shot up, and a rights issue to develop the find brought half a million pounds flooding into the company. Mark Ashford was launched on a new career in the stockmarket.

Unhappily, the mine never really lived up to its initial potential and an underground fire burnt out many of the drives and shafts that had been added. With half the cash from the rights issue still unspent and a £200,000 insurance payment from an inflated fire claim, Ashford set about building up a mining conglomerate to share in the rich spoils being yielded in South Africa.

He called his company South African Mining and planned its growth by the surreptitious purchase of controlling interests in mining companies whose stockmarket capitalization on the Johannesburg stock exchange did not fully value the mining assets of the company involved.

Behind every deal he did, there lay the same old pattern of fraud that started with the early reconstruction of his grandmother's finances. Behind the impressive facade of accounts, publicity handouts, write-ups in the city pages, every deal had that same old delectable three-card trick. The money disappeared. It ended, by various tortuous routes, in Mark Ashford's numbered account in the main branch of the Union Bank of Switzerland in Zurich.

In recent years, the steady flow of funds pouring into the Union Bank account all had one thing in common. They had all been made in the stockmarkets of London, New York and Johannesburg and they had all involved ripping off the general public in one form or another – rights issues, takeovers, bogus new discoveries, every one accompanied by a great story.

Mark Ashford had got fraud down to a fine art. He knew how to milk the investing public and he knew how to do it legally. So long as there were investors around prepared to put up the hard cash for a share in his companies' future aspirations and profits, Mark Ashford always found a deal. The schemes only occasionally materialized, but there was always a bigger and juicier deal around the corner, so the money kept pumping in. Mark Ashford used to call it 'feeding the ducks'.

Each morning, before he left for South African Mining's office in the city, he stood by the pond in front of his Berkshire mansion and fed the rare red and gold Chinese ducks he kept there. They never ceased to fascinate him. Each time he threw a piece of bread, the ducks fought and squawked over it. Every time they wanted more, they quacked loudly at him. Sometimes, he withheld the bread and just watched them quacking. They reminded him of investors.

Now forty-two and a millionaire many times over, Mark Ashford was a master in providing for that insatiable appetite stockmarket punters have for making fast money. He was the merchant of their dreams. When the ducks quacked on the stockmarkets of London, Johannesburg and New York, Mark Ashford was always there to feed them.

15

London
Monday 19 September
8.30 p.m.

'Gentlemen,' said Mark Ashford, swirling a Campari around the thick cut glass in his right hand, 'Someone has let the cat out of the bag.

'Eastern Mining jumped from nine cents to twenty-nine cents today in Johannesburg on rumours that we had a new strike at Amanda. Nearly a million shares changed hands and some bright spark has snapped up ten per cent of the company.'

The three men sat at a corner table in the main restaurant at the Savoy hotel, just off London's Strand. They were all directors of South African Mining, the third largest mining conglomerate in South Africa, controlled from New York and London by Mark Ashford and his family trusts.

Although there were seven other directors on the main board, these three were the triumvirate who made the important policy decisions.

Ashford sat opposite his two other directors, ex-merchant banker, Hamish Macfarlane and Jack Plane. Plane was the first to break the silence.

'Does it really matter? We are all large shareholders in Eastern Mining. If the shares rocket we make money with the rest of them.' He swallowed half a glass of whisky in one long gulp and signalled the waiter for another.

Mark Ashford eyed him without showing obvious concern. He couldn't rely on Jack's judgement any more. Ever since he started drinking heavily there had been blind spots in his decision making. The sharp business intellect that impressed Ashford when he had first met him eight years earlier had been steadily blunted over the years by whisky. Had they not been friends for so long, and had

Jack not known so much, Mark Ashford would have kicked him off the board a while ago.

'Wake up, Jack,' he said, with a smile. 'We've spent one and a half million of South African Mining's money developing one of the richest gold deposits in southern Africa without a word to shareholders. That's fraud in anyone's language. What's more we've spent South African Mining's money on a virtually dormant mining shell we do not control – and which we want to buy out privately for ourselves. The very last thing we want is any comment anywhere about Eastern Mining and Amanda.'

'Yes, quite,' said Jack quietly and sipped at his new whisky.

'What is so damn annoying,' continued Ashford, 'is that in another few days we could have bought the whole lot for twelve cents a share ourselves. I signed the papers yesterday to buy the two farms around Amanda's· lease area. They are going into a new company called Southern Zimbabwe Farms, which will be owned in Switzerland by us. Southern Zimbabwe Farms will then make a nominal bid for Eastern Mining. The only names that will appear anywhere are the Union Bank of Switzerland nominees.'

'But, Mark, Jack's right to an extent. We are all shareholders of Eastern Mining. We can't lose.'

Mark Ashford scowled at both his directors in turn.

'I don't believe you two. For years we have slaved away building up South African Mining, primarily for the benefit of shareholders. Now comes a chance to make a fortune on our own account, and you two suddenly start moralizing.' Mark Ashford was getting heated. 'Don't you see, buying out Eastern Mining is our great chance. From the borehole results so far, Amanda has got more high-grade gold than any other mine in Zimbabwe. Even at the present price of $450 there is over three hundred million rands' worth of fucking gold down there.'

The head waiter appeared and they ordered dinner.

'Well, where do we go from here?' asked Hamish Macfarlane. 'It's going to be hard to stop speculation, particularly if it's another mining house doing the buying.'

'I don't think it is,' said Ashford. 'I checked with Max. It seems to be two local brokers acting on their own. Izzie Van Royen and Eddie Vandermeer. Van Royen is a hard-nosed market trader – runs his own broking firm. Vandermeer is much younger. A partner in his father's firm Vandermeer & Vandermeer. If it was another mining group they would use one of the big brokers. What we must do is kill the speculation and get the share price down. There are a number of alternatives.'

They discussed various approaches to the problem for an hour, analysing cause and effect all the way down the line.

Finally, Ashford summed up the plan of action. 'We'll issue a statement at Eastern Mining's annual general meeting in two days, saying we are doing some routine prospecting at Amanda before selling the land as grazing. That will cover us in case anyone flies over the mine and sees the new buildings and shafts. I'll order a fresh clampdown on security both at the mine and in the Johannesburg office.

'South African Mining owns thirty-five per cent of Eastern Mining which gives us some two million shares to play with. As soon as the announcement's been made, we'll flood the market with 500,000 Eastern Mining shares through three or four brokers. If that doesn't knock the stuffing out of the share price, I don't know what will.'

'Who else knows about those borehole results?' asked Hamish Macfarlane.

'Fred Spillman and his surveyor in Johannesburg, and the three of us. The originals of the drilling survey are in my safe here in London. Not even the mine manager knows the real story. He has been given specially doctored maps and ore grades. He won't find out the truth until it's too late. Then I'll buy him off.'

He turned to Jack Plane. 'I want you to go out to Johannesburg on the first available flight and supervise the share sales after the AGM. Also work on a statement for the meeting. Keep in close touch with me on the phone and observe strict security – no calls through switchboards.'

They left the Savoy at 10.30 p.m. Driving home to his Berkshire estate in the back of his Silver Shadow, Mark Ashford remained deep in thought about Eastern Mining.

His position was secure. Only he knew exactly what the new mine was worth. Anyone else would be guessing. If need be, he would sell South African Mining's entire holding – over two million shares - in the market. It would rain Eastern Mining stock for days. He would hammer the share price into the ground with wave after wave of selling. Even the most persistent buyer would be deterred.

No one was going to dictate to Mark Ashford. Those days were over a long time ago.

16

Johannesburg
Wednesday 28 September
5.30 p.m.

At last publication day for the annual report, and accounts of Eastern Mining had arrived. It had only been a few days since Eddie and Izzie bought their stakes in Eastern Mining, but for Eddie, with his larger position, the wait seemed an eternity. The burst of excitement in the market caused by their buying spree and the subsequent press speculation about Amanda's prospects had been doused in the days that followed by the sale of large lines of Eastern Mining shares.

The market in Eastern Mining suddenly became water-logged with stock. The selling was organized through the three largest firms, and after careful inquiry on the trading floor and in the members' bar, Eddie had been told the selling emanated from London. There was little doubt in his mind, and absolute conviction in Izzie's, that Mark Ashford was behind it.

The powerful mining houses are experts at killing off unwanted speculation, and a favourite way is simply to unload shares. It was not the first time Eddie had seen a mining house 'operating' a stock before making an important announcement, and in the tough mining camp atmosphere of the Johannesburg stockmarket, it was a common enough ploy. The simple logic is that if the stock was that good the main shareholder wouldn't be selling. On the contrary, he would be buying.

At first, the Eastern Mining price held steady as punters snapped up the shares, but as the selling built up, the share price started to fall. The first few trades were done at forty cents, then the price fell steadily to twenty-four cents. For a share that had only been eleven cents a few days earlier, the fall was not dramatic and a lot of those who bought early on were still showing handsome profits. But for those who bought around the thirty cent mark a sagging price of twenty-four cents left a slightly sick, sinking feeling.

Not, however, for Eddie. Although he was anxious for the news of the new mine to be released, he was confident about Eastern Mining's prospects and was able to sit back and take a relatively detached view of the situation. The memory of those new shafts, the headgear, the newly bulldozed dirt roads stretching out into the Amanda lease area, the construction of a new refinery, and the miners' sleeping quarters, burnt bright in his mind.

Shortly after the market closed at 3.30 p.m., Eddie took the elevator up to the second-floor general office of the exchange to see if the Eastern Mining accounts had arrived. It is practice for companies reporting financial statements to send copies to the general office for distribution to member broking firms. Eddie hoped to short-cut the system and collect his own copy, instead of waiting for it to be stuck in Vandermeer & Vandermeer's pigeonhole next morning.

He strolled into the general office and was immediately confronted with the man he hoped to meet least, Doug Davies, the short, fat, bald clerk to the committee who was the major domo of the general office. Like the president, Doug Davies was a Welshman, and, also like the president, had inherited all the stealth and cunning of his marauding forefathers from the green, rain-sodden hills of Wales.

Doug Davies was one of the few men in the stock exchange Eddie actively disliked. Most people, he found, had some redeeming features, but Doug Davies had none. Even his soft, lilting, Welsh accent was spoilt by a natural sneer.

Eddie's feelings were also shared by his father. Four years earlier, while serving on the stock-exchange committee, William Vandermeer had opposed Doug Davies's appointment. He didn't like the man's manner and trusted him even less. William Vandermeer's opposition to the appointment was an open secret and he never hid his feelings when talking with friends and colleagues.

But Davies had a powerful job. The clerk to the stock-exchange committee has official access to every sphere of stock-exchange life, including the state of a broker's finances, and membership. He also advises and polices the various financial statements a public company is required to make from time to time, monitors trading situations in the market, and, where necessary, advises on the required action to comply with stock-exchange rules. His source of power in all these matters is the backing and authority of the council. Doug Davies was, therefore, a man almost permanently on the inside track. His advice was constantly sought by harassed managing directors and finance directors who had lost their way, or had knowingly broken the complicated and often contradictory rules of the Johannesburg stock exchange.

The rule book was only really understood by a handful of men, mostly officials and the legal department. Very few industrialists ever took the time to plough through it themselves. It was easier to pick up the phone and speak to the exchange's own oracle.

'Thought you'd be up here quick,' smiled Doug Davies. He lifted a set of accounts from the top of the pile beside him and tossed it onto the long desk in front of Eddie.

'Getting itchy feet?' he said. 'I see Eastern Mining have fallen away sharply. Did I see them at twenty-four cents?'

'It's about to double. You ought to get a few.' Eddie gave him a knowing wink. 'Or would that be insider dealing?' He didn't wait for a reply. He picked up the accounts, tapped them twice on the desk and left.

Eddie walked round to Izzie Van Royen's office, a few minutes away, reading snatches from the accounts as he went. He flicked through the chairman's annual statement and found what he was looking for second paragraph from the end. Then he started running. He didn't have a moment to lose. He leapt up the stone grey stairway to Izzie's office two and three steps at a time.

Izzie was stretched out in his old leather swivel chair, long legs crossed on the end of his desk.

'Read this,' said Eddie, dropping the accounts in front of him.

Izzie sat bolt upright. 'Help yourself to a beer,' he said. Eddie took a couple of cans from the fridge, ripped the tops and passed one to Izzie.

'Now we'll see what these bastards have been up to,' said Izzie, taking a long swig.

He turned to the chairman's statement and read aloud.

During the course of the year, exploration activity has been taking place around the lease area of the Amanda mine to establish whether there were sufficiently interesting ore grades to allow us to re-open the mine on an operational basis.

Izzie underlined the words 're-open' and 'operational'.

Eddie was surprised at how slowly and hesitantly he read. Here was a man with one of the sharpest trading intellects he had encountered, yet he read like a child.

At first the results proved encouraging, but as I have pointed out in previous statements, the ore body at Amanda is badly faulted and after an intensive drilling programme your directors are of the opinion that there is no chance of re-opening the old Amanda mine on a profitable basis.

'You know what they're trying to do?' interrupted Eddie.

'I know boy, I know,' laughed Izzie. 'It's not the first

time a mining house has tried to rip off minority shareholders – and it won't be the last.' He returned to the text.

Although this is disappointing, we have in the last few weeks
received an offer for Eastern Mining, which the poor drilling
results have forced us to consider. A neighbouring Zimbabwean
cattle-ranching company wants extra ranching land for their
cattle-rearing activities. Shareholders will receive details of the
offer in the next few days.

'They can't get away with this, can they? We've seen the
mine, we've got the maps, the ore grades.'
    'No, they bloody well can't. But they don't know that
yet!' Izzie picked up the Eastern Mining accounts and
stuffed them into a worn leather briefcase. Then he looked
at Eddie, a disturbing seriousness crossed his falcon-like
features.
    'They're all crooked, man,' he said, his Afrikaans accent
clipping the word 'crooked'. 'The whole system is crooked.
You could buy any one of those committee members for a
five-rand note. And the mining houses are the biggest
bloody thieves of the lot. They've been ripping off minority
shareholders for years.' He stood up briefcase in hand.
'Come on, let's get out of here. We'll make a plan tomorrow
for the meeting. We've got three days.'

The annual general meeting of Eastern Mining was normally a sedate affair, a non-event on the financial calendar,
attended by the directors of Eastern Mining and a few old
diehards, retired employees, and miners who remembered
the glorious days of Amanda's past with affection. As the
mine had been on a care and maintenance basis for so
long, there was never anything interesting to report to
shareholders. A public company has a legal requirement
to hold an annual general meeting once a year, and it was
in this spirit of compulsory need that the meetings took
place. The annual accounts were rubber stamped and questions rarely asked; the meeting was normally over in ten
minutes.

81

This year, however, the annual general meeting of Eastern Mining won five-star billing.

Public interest in the meeting was ensured by the recent controversy and the heavy trading that took place in Eastern Mining on the London, New York and Johannesburg stockmarkets immediately before the meeting. It was the most actively traded gold share in all of the big markets and a virtual tug of war developed over the price, as wave after wave of selling knocked the price down and occasional stampedes of buying pushed it back up again. Leading the pack of buyers in Johannesburg were Eddie and Izzie. Between them, they had the Johannesburg market sewn up.

Not content with his existing holding, the gambler in Eddie had got the better of him. He simply could not resist increasing his holding in a share he knew was about to double, treble, quadruple from its current price of twenty-six cents. It was the sort of stock you could put your house on, and that is exactly what Eddie did.

He went along to the head office of Central Merchant Bank, Vandermeer's bankers for more than twenty years and borrowed half a million rand. In return for the money, the bank held the shares as collateral for the loan and asked for the deeds of Eddie's house as extra protection against a sudden market fall.

He asked his father's permission before raising the loan, and though the amount was larger than William Vandermeer had ever borrowed, he agreed. There are very few times in a stockmarket career when a sure-fire winner presents itself, and although he was more cautious than his son, William Vandermeer recognized the upside potential.

Armed with his half-million Eddie went back into the market and started buying aggressively. When the selling knocked the price down, Eddie started buying, or sometimes Izzie bought for him. It was now widely assumed, after all the stories and publicity, that Eastern Mining would be making some sort of statement at the annual general meeting and Eddie's buying encouraged the other punters.

Activity in the stock was hectic and Izzie, always a delight to watch when operating in a moving stock, was in his element. Sometimes he was a buyer, sometimes he was a seller. His adversaries on the trading floor never really knew which way he was going to move.

The uproar the pair created with their tactics, the big dipper rises and falls created by their buying and Mark Ashford's selling during the run-up to the meeting guaranteed intense interest from everybody – investors, newspapers, other mining houses and even the committee of the Johannesburg stock exchange. Eastern Mining was the talk of the financial town, the stock of the day in the bars and restaurants around Hollard Street. And now the big day had arrived.

Eddie and Izzie stood in the long queue of shareholders waiting to have their Eastern Mining share certificates, proof of their right to attend the meeting, vetted by a posse of tense-looking Eastern Mining executives swarming around the ornately carved wooden doors into the large ground-floor boardroom at Eastern Mining's headquarters.

Both men had dressed for the occasion. Eddie was dressed in a double-breasted navy silk suit, white shirt and blue and red striped Dior tie. His blond hair, neatly parted, fell long at the back, touching the top of his jacket collar. He felt in good spirits and was relaxed about the outcome of the meeting. This time there had to be a statement.

After all the speculation and constant press attention, no board of directors would dare ignore the situation. And, of course, there was always question time at the end of the meeting, the one time of the year when shareholders can quiz directors about developments and have a legal right to a proper answer. There is, as with many of the more important stock-exchange rules, an acknowledged grey area, where a company chairman can argue that releasing certain information for public consumption was not in the company's interest, but Eddie could not see how that provision applied. The discovery and development of a rich new ore body in a defunct mine had to be good news for everybody.

Izzie stood beside him, looking every bit as dapper, but his was a different kind of smartness – his own special brand. His oiled silver-grey hair was swept back off his forehead, impeccably combed and he wore a dark brown cotton suit, white shirt and a wide yellow and brown paisley tie.

Izzie handed both their share certificates to the official at the entrance. The man checked them against a list of names and numbers.

'Vandermeer or Van Royen? Which are you?' he asked Izzie officiously, handing back the certificates.

'Van Royen. And don't you forget it. You'll be hearing a lot more from me.'

'Thank you Mr Van Royen,' the man said and looked away.

'Don't mention it,' replied Izzie curtly, and he and Eddie walked into the meeting.

Izzie's mood changed almost immediately. The atmosphere was charged with the excitement that surrounds big money and controversy and Izzie sensed an air of carnival among the rows of smartly dressed brokers, shareholders, and financial journalists who filled the lines of chairs in the hall. They walked slowly down to the front row, stopping every now and then to shake hands with a client, or greet a friend from the market.

'Will they say anything Mr Vandermeer?' asked an elderly man with grey hair.

'If they don't there'll be trouble,' smiled Eddie. 'Are you a shareholder, sir?'

'Yes. I worked on the mine in the good old days. I've had my shares fifteen years.'

'Don't sell them now. They've got a brand new mine up there.' Eddie shook hands with the man. 'Come and see me if I can be of help to you.'

'Thank you, I'll remember that.'

As they settled into their seats Jack Plane and a line of Eastern Mining executives walked into the hall and up side steps to a raised stage. They sat down at a long table and the roar of conversation evaporated to a low drone. Bill

Borden, the Eastern Mining chairman, took the middle of the table. He waited patiently for a pause among the coughing, paper rattling and chair moving before he began. Then he stood up and tapped the green baize table top lightly with a polished wooden hammer. The room fell silent.

'Ladies and gentlemen, perhaps we could make a start. First of all let me say how pleased I am to see that this meeting is so well attended. It's a long time since we've seen such a distinguished crowd.'

He paused, took off his glasses, and smiled at the audience.

'As you are no doubt all aware, your company has suddenly jumped into the limelight both in terms of trading activity on the stockmarket and the headlines of the financial press. These are all matters we shall be dealing with later on in the meeting.'

'Thank Christ for that,' said Eddie in a stage whisper to Izzie, and a ripple of laughter broke out in the seats around them.

'But first of all let me introduce you to Jack Plane, an executive director of your company and managing director of Eastern Mining's largest shareholder, South African Mining. Mr Plane was in Johannesburg, and agreed to attend this meeting. I will go through this year's report and accounts, and perhaps then I could pass you over to Mr Plane who has an announcement to make.'

Cheering and applause broke out from the back of the hall. Bill Borden lifted his hand and hammered the baize table top to bring the meeting to order.

'Please, please,' he shouted above the din. 'I must caution you against believing the wildly optimistic stories circulating the stockmarket and some financial pages.' He opened his palms to the crowd in a papal gesture of conciliation and his voice assumed a firm, convincing tone.

'While we do have some good news for you later on in the meeting, I fear it might fall short of many expectations.' Bill Borden sounded as if he genuinely believed what he was saying.

But Eddie remained unperturbed. Any 'good news' would help the share price. Mining houses were always the same about new strikes, if they weren't deliberately secretive they were certainly cautious. Often they were not sure of the size of the strike until the drilling and development programmes were completed, while the problems in constructing underground workings, the sinking of shafts and the tunnelling out of cross sections and driveways, so miners could reach the rich seams, were many and varied.

As most experienced investors in the gold market knew, often to their cost, it's one thing to find gold – and quite another to get it out of the ground profitably.

For the next thirty-five minutes Bill Borden went painstakingly through every significant item of the accounts. He was under instructions from Mark Ashford to be thorough, there was to be no reason for criticism. No questions were asked and the only interruption was the odd bout of coughing.

Eventually, Bill Borden reached the end of the accounts and introduced Jack Plane. The hall hushed again with anticipation as he stood up. His long, lean body was well tailored in light grey flannel and his cream shirt and army tie set off his suntan. There was no sign of the lonely bouts of drinking that had become an increasingly important part of his life. Last night it had started at midnight in the ground-floor bar of the Carlton hotel and then into the early hours alone in his bedroom till he had fallen asleep, the empty bottle of Scotch still in his hand when he awoke.

'First let me say,' he started off briskly, 'how delighted I am to be here in Johannesburg. I hope what I have to say will bring to a close the intense press speculation and heavy trading of Eastern Mining in the world's stockmarkets.' Jack Plane paused to pour a glass of water and took a sip.

'As you all know, Eastern Mining's gold mine in Zimbabwe has been run on a care and maintenance basis for some years now. Last year, your board decided that there was little point in continuing to pay the high level of costs required to maintain the mine unless there was a very substantial rise in the gold price. This has not so far been forthcoming. The low and patchy ore grades at Amanda would require a gold price of at least seven hundred dollars before it would be worth returning them into full production again.'

Jack Plane surveyed his audience. He seemed to be pitching it at the right level and they listened with rapt attention.

'Even the rise in the gold price over the past few days to 450 dollars makes the possibility remote at best. Three months ago your directors decided to instigate a full programme of exploratory drilling to try and establish whether it was worth maintaining the mine. We have drilled most of the Amanda lease area and the results of that drilling programme are not very encouraging. While initial ore samples contained quite surprisingly high grades of gold, these values subsequently petered out and the results for the majority of the lease area were at best mediocre and very patchy.'

He paused for a moment to let the news sink in. 'We still have more drilling to do, and of course we will keep you posted, but in the light of the current situation, your directors have had to look more seriously at an offer by a local Zimbabwe ranching company who want to buy the Amanda leases for additional cattle grazing. That approach has been put into a formal offer, copies of which will be given to you after this meeting. The offer values each Eastern Mining share at twenty cents. While this is not as much as the stockmarket seems to think they are worth – I think the price is around thirty cents today – it does represent a very considerable increase on the share price before the recent speculation. The acceptance date for the offer, as you will see when you receive your copies, is in three weeks' time and there will be a meeting of shareholders before then to vote on the offer.

'I can tell you that in the light of current drilling results your board, having examined the full circumstances of the offer, are recommending shareholders to accept and will be voting in favour of it with their thirty-six per cent shareholding.'

He smiled at his audience. 'If anyone has a question, I'll be very happy to help where I can.'

The hall roared its discontent. That was not what shareholders had been expecting. A twenty-cent takeover bid was not the gold bonanza most of them had been banking on. When the news hit the stockmarket, the shares would slump from thirty to twenty cents, the value of the offer. A big drop from the forty-six cents Eddie paid for some of his shares, and an even nastier percentage.

Eddie turned to Izzie. 'That's theft in anyone's language.'

'Don't worry, man,' grinned Izzie. 'We've got 'em cooked.'

The tall straight figure of Izzie Van Royen rose to his feet and the noise died away.

'My name is Van Royen,' he said. 'I wonder, Mr Plane, if I might ask you a question?'

'Of course.'

'Would you be so kind to tell us the name of the ranching company that has made this offer?'

'Yes, certainly. The company is Southern Zimbabwe Ranching. It owns substantial tracts of grazing land around the Amanda mining lease area.'

'Thank you,' said Izzie. 'And can you tell me Mr Plane, please, who owns Southern Zimbabwe?'

'Yes, I can. So far as I'm aware, the company is owned by a group of investors – Swiss nationals.' Jack Plane realized his mistake as soon as he'd said it.

'When you say "Swiss nationals",' said Izzie, seizing on the point, 'do you mean Swiss nominees?'

'Well . . .' for a moment Jack Plane hesitated, 'I haven't met them personally and to the best of my knowledge negotiations have been conducted through their bank.'

'Is that a Swiss bank or a local Zimbabwe bank?' Now Izzie's voice had a threatening edge to it.

'I believe both were involved.'

'Thank you, Mr Plane. That is very interesting. Please

make sure our conversation is recorded in the official minutes of this meeting. I shall make my own note of the matter.'

'Certainly. And if you need more detailed information perhaps I could have a word with you afterwards.'

'That would be most kind.' And with that Izzie sat down.

A few other shareholders asked questions, and within ten minutes the meeting was closed. Izzie and Eddie made straight for Jack Plane.

'All right, Plane, where do we talk?'

'Ah! Mr Van Royen, yes . . .' He turned to Eddie 'And Mr . . . ?'

'Vandermeer.'

'How about the anteroom,' he said, pointing to a door halfway down the hall. 'We won't be disturbed there.'

In the small, windowless conference parlour the three men stood facing each other.

'All right, Plane, what's going on?' demanded Izzie.

Jack Plane looked startled. No one had spoken to him like that for a long time.

'Please I do think we should try to keep this meeting . . .'

Izzie grabbed him by the lapels of his jacket.

'Then I'll say it nice and politely,' he said, glaring down at the smaller man.

Eddie stood there watching. He was getting more and more disenchanted with Izzie's style of campaign. He didn't disapprove of the strong-arm approach when all else failed, but Izzie's method of immediate confrontation excluded any other possibility. Plane might be innocent and let some information slip accidentally; he might dislike his job, or hate Mark Ashford. Though Eddie liked many things about Izzie, his tactics had their distinct limitations.

'Now you run and tell Mark Ashford,' continued Izzie, 'we know all about his new mine at Amanda and this whole crooked takeover deal. He has one hour to make us an offer for our shares. And I mean an offer that reflects the true value of Amanda. I'll be waiting at my office.'

89

'But . . .'

'One hour. Or I'll teach that son of a bitch a lesson he'll never forget.'

17

An hour came and went and there was no phone call. Eddie and Izzie sat in Izzie's office reading the small print in the Eastern Mining offer document. They had finished the few cans of beer, so they drank whisky and water. As both men expected, the new prospect at Amanda was not mentioned.

'I think it's about time we pulled the rug from under Ashford's feet,' said Izzie. 'He's had long enough.' He picked up the phone book on his desk and flicked through the pages till he found the main Rand Reserve Bank number in Rissik Street. He dialled and asked for the bank's chairman David Maltby.

'Chairman's office,' answered an icy female voice.

'Mr Maltby please. My name is Van Royen. I'd like to speak to him about a mistake in the Eastern Mining offer document.'

'Yes, Mr Van Royen.' David Maltby was on the line a few moments later.

'Mr Maltby, you have signed on behalf of Rand Reserve Bank that the offer document for Eastern Mining represents a fair deal for minority shareholders.'

'That is correct.'

'Well, I have documents in my possession that might make you want to retract that statement.'

David Maltby laughed nervously. 'That would be extremely embarrassing.'

'I could bring the documents over right now.'

There was a slight pause, then David Maltby said, 'If you're serious, Mr Van Royen, I think you'd better.'

'I'll be there in five minutes.'

* * *

90

The names Eddie Vandermeer and Izzie Van Royen meant little to David Maltby, but he welcomed both men warmly. His office had all the charm of a private hospital waiting room. The walls were white, the desk, chairs and wall cupboards were made of tubular steel and polished veneer, a silver paperweight lay on a clean white blotter, and the low hiss of the air conditioner replenished the room with sanitized air.

Maltby was a career banker with all the ease and confidence of a man who had reached the height of his profession quickly. He leant across the sparkling glass-topped desk that dominated his office and pushed a button on the intercom.

'No calls for fifteen minutes.' He didn't wait for a reply.

'Perhaps I should start with some background detail,' said Eddie.

'Please do.' David Maltby settled into his large, leather, executive chair looking unperturbed, but inside he felt uneasy and concerned. The idea that his bank had signed an incorrect financial statement on a public document made him shiver.

'Mr Van Royen and I are minority shareholders in Eastern Mining and own some twenty per cent of the company. It is in this capacity we have come to see you.'

Izzie was grim-faced, his eyes were scornful. He disliked all types of officialdom and had a special distrust of bankers.

'I see,' said Maltby, glancing at Izzie.

'The reason we bought,' continued Eddie, 'is that on a recent trip to Zimbabwe we visited the Amanda mine and found, much to our surprise, a significant amount of construction work in progress. There were new shafts, roads, a refining plant . . . you don't have to be a genius to know what that means.'

'No quite,' David Maltby cleared his throat with a nervous cough. 'Let's be clear about this. If I understand you correctly, you are saying the Amanda has a new mining potential which has not been disclosed.'

'We go further than that.' Izzie joined the discussion.

Bankers, brokers, fund managers, he thought, they were all the same – motivated by personal gain. 'We are saying the whole deal is a fraud, signed and approved by your bank.'

'Of course you wouldn't come to my office and make statements like that unless you had some proof?'

Eddie opened his briefcase and laid the two aerial photos of the mine alongside each other on David Maltby's gleaming glass-topped desk.

'You can see quite clearly, this bright area here is desert scrubland with buildings on it.' He pointed to the same areas on the next photograph. 'And here we have two lines of dark shadow, the new buildings. These two spots here are the new shafts.'

David Maltby inspected both photographs closely. He took a large, white-handled magnifying glass from his desk draw and scrutinized the shadows. The evidence, he decided, was not conclusive. Shadows there were, but from these pictures he could not identify them as a new mine.

'Is that all there is?' he asked.

The note of reproachment was too much for Izzie. He felt the anger rising. 'Don't be such a bloody idiot,' he shouted at David Maltby, as he stood up. He walked over to Maltby's desk and leant heavily on the front of it. 'What do you mean is that all there is?' he repeated menacingly. 'Who do you think you are? Your bank has signed a public document valuing a new gold mine as cattle grazing and you start talking down to us like we're managers reporting to management. You and your fucking bank are in all sorts of trouble, so don't you start taking high-handed attitudes with me.'

'Now please I must insist . . .'

'Shut up and listen.' He slammed a fist down on Maltby's desk. 'You've got forty-eight hours to withdraw your bank's name from that offer document or I'm going to the police.'

Izzie pointed an accusing finger. 'You'll end up in the slammer – and you can kiss your bank goodbye.' Izzie was shouting now. 'Get off your fat banker's arse Mr Maltby, or they'll lock you up and throw away the key.'

He turned to leave. 'I'll wait for you at home,' he said to Eddie on his way out, and slammed the door with a resounding crash.

David Maltby stared after him blankly.

'Did I say something?' he asked Eddie eventually.

'I don't think so. I'm sorry, he runs on a very short fuse.'

David Maltby still looked shaken. 'Now where were we . . . yes, the photos . . .'

'There's more,' said Eddie. He unfurled his copy of the map taken from the Amanda office and spread it out. 'This is a detailed plan of the drilling programme, with individual borehole results. You can follow the line of the new deposit from the grades of each borehole.' Eddie circled a line of borehole results that stretched across the map and the small hand-printed figures beside each one. 'Look at these grades, fourteen grams a ton, sixteen . . . some of the best results I've ever seen.'

David Maltby inspected the map closely. Some of the grades shown were excellent, and as far as he could remember the line of drilling was authentic.

The results appeared to trace a rich vein of ore starting off to one side of the old mine workings and running out to the perimeter of the lease area.

'Where did you get this map, Mr Vandermeer?'

'I can't tell you. But I assure you it's genuine.'

'Can I borrow it . . . and the photos?' He did not expect to get them but thought it worth a try.

'I'm afraid not. Mr Van Royen and I have decided not to let them out of our sight. But if you need them, I'll bring them wherever you want.'

David Maltby was worried, but his professional cool did not desert him.

'Fine,' he said. 'Well, I don't need to tell you the consequences for this bank if your information is correct. If you'll excuse me, I have a great deal of checking to do.'

As soon as he had shown Eddie out, he picked up the phone.

* * *

Eddie arrived home to find Izzie and Lucy sitting by the pool having a drink. Izzie had considerable charm with women, though few men ever saw that side of him.

'We've been waiting for you.' She smiled and kissed him lightly on the cheek. 'White wine or beer,' she asked. 'They're both cold.'

'Just what I need,' he said, loosening his tie and unbuttoning his shirt. 'White wine, lots of ice.'

He sat down on the canvas chair and stretched his legs. There was an uneasy silence. Izzie inhaled deeply from his cigarette and blew a plume of blue smoke through the still evening air. Both men looked out across the pool. The birds in the delphinium bushes were in full voice and Eddie heard a car sweep past the end of the garden on its way down Second Avenue.

Eddie broke the tension. 'Why did you behave like that with Maltby? What was the point?'

Izzie looked at him disdainfully. 'Don't tell me how to run my affairs.'

Eddie knew he was treading on dangerous ground, but their relationship could not continue the way it was.

'Fine. But why upset people? Maltby might be a useful ally.'

'Don't be a bloody idiot. Ashford's one of his biggest clients. He's been taking money from him for years.'

'You don't know that,' said Eddie sharply. 'It's just an assumption like all the others.'

'Don't push me, Eddie,' Izzie threatened.

'I'm not. But I can't go along with this continual confrontation. I don't believe the only way to treat people is to crack them over the head with a pickaxe handle.'

Izzie stood up. 'So all of a sudden, Mr Clever Dick, you know all the answers.' Izzie was shouting now. 'You know how I should treat people, how I should talk to them. I've been in this game a lot longer than you, boy. If you don't like the way I operate, that's your problem. I don't need you or anyone else.'

Izzie picked up his briefcase to leave, and Eddie blocked his path.

'Get out of my way.'

'Now look. I don't want to fall out with you . . .'

'I told you to get out of my way.'

'Hear me out,' said Eddie, not shifting.

Izzie's eyes narrowed.

'You're a friend. We got into this together,' said Eddie.

'I won't tell you again. Out of my way.' He pushed past Eddie and marched across the lawn to his car.

Eddie watched him reverse the big maroon Buick and accelerate hard down the drive.

'What was that all about?' asked Lucy. She stood behind him, a glass of wine in each hand. 'I could hear the shouting from the kitchen.'

'He's impossible.'

'I thought you two were friends?' Lucy passed him a glass. 'We are. But every time someone upsets him, he wants to beat the daylights out of them. Anyway, let's forget about him. It's not important.'

They sat on the sunlounger sipping their wine, Lucy curled up beside him.

'Mother phoned tonight,' she said. 'Daddy's coming to Johannesburg on business next week for a few days. She said they would stay here and look after the girls if we wanted the house. Can we go?'

Lucy's parents lived in a beach house an hour's drive north of Durban, in the heart of the rolling green sugar plantations covering that part of the coastline. The house was built into the rocks overlooking the Indian Ocean, and had its own small private beach and jetty. Her father, a keen sailor and ex-naval commander, owned a fine white wood sloop.

The idea appealed to Eddie, though he wondered if it was wise to leave Johannesburg. But there was a phone down there and his father could keep an eye on Eastern Mining.

'Could we use the boat?' he asked.

'Of course. It's ready to go. Dad says we should sail up the coast for a couple of days. Friends of theirs have a hotel there.'

Lucy's hand touched his shoulder. 'Come on,' she said. 'Be fun. Get you out of this place for a while.'

'You're right. I haven't been much fun lately, have I? We can catch the ten o'clock flight to Durban on Saturday morning.'

Lucy put her arms round Eddie and kissed him. 'Mmm,' she said, 'I love you.'

A long black chauffeur-driven Mercedes swept quietly down the drive and stopped in front of the house. Eddie recognized the trim figure of David Maltby stepping from the car and went over to meet him.

'How did you find me?' he asked.

'Telephone book. You're the only Vandermeer in Houghton so I took a chance.'

'Come and have a drink,' said Eddie.

'Love to,' replied David Maltby, smiling, 'but another time. I have a meeting at 2.30 tomorrow afternoon with the local South African Mining people. Could you bring your photos and maps? We shall have to tread carefully – they're major clients. But you own twenty per cent of the company and have a right to hear their reaction. I'll have to ask you to keep a pretty low profile though.'

'No problem.'

'And you'll come alone. I don't think we need a floorshow from Mr Van Royen.'

'Understood.'

'Good. Then my office at 2.30 p.m.'

18

Mark Ashford paced around his Manhattan penthouse in a silk dressing gown drinking his third cup of coffee of the morning. He didn't understand it. Fred Spillman, the man in charge of his South African mining operations had suddenly disappeared. For ten years he had never failed to get hold of Fred day or night, but three times in the last two weeks Fred Spillman had disappeared.

David Maltby's call had woken him an hour earlier. He had to speak to Spillman, but he was nowhere to be found.

He wasn't at the Johannesburg head office, nor his favourite bar at the top of the Carlton hotel, or any of the three restaurants he used for lunch. Mark Ashford had telephoned them all. It was a mystery – even his secretary didn't understand. 'I'm sorry,' she told him, 'he just seems to have vanished.' Mark Ashford checked his watch. It was 1.30 p.m. in Johannesburg. Lunch time. There was one number he hadn't tried.

Fred Spillman stretched out on the navy blue mattress of the white wooden sunbed and moved his head a little to one side to catch the full heat of the sun on his face. Through the steady, icy trickle of the swimming-pool fountain beside him, he felt the harsh African sun gently easing the sweat from his body. Rivulets ran down his chest and arms.

He leant over to the small table beside him and poured himself another tumbler of Black Label and added some ice. He took two long gulps, rolled an ice cube around his mouth, and spat it back into the glass. At times like this, he thought, it was all worth while – all the lying, the cheating, the constant manipulating of people to do what he wanted.

Although Wednesday was normally a busy day at the South African Mining headquarters on Market Street, Fred Spillman was having lunch at home. Or to be more precise, lunch without his wife. It started two weeks ago when he introduced the new maid Clarissa, into the family. He met her by chance in Clowes, the big department store at the Carlton Centre, where she worked on the men's toiletries counter. She was a stunningly beautiful Cape coloured and Fred Spillman was captivated by her immediately.

Two days after his first visit, he was back. Within a week he had bought four bottles of aftershave. On the fourth visit he brought her a present, a gold watch in a black velvet box. Clarissa accepted knowingly.

'If you need a maid I will come and work for you.'

It was deliciously simple. He turned and gazed into her

97

dark, sultry eyes and to his amazement, she winked at him. There was an employment agency where his wife had a permanent order for good home staff, and two weeks later Clarissa was their new maid.

That morning at breakfast the plan had been laid as he sat sipping coffee and reading the business section of the *Rand Daily Mail*.

'Clarissa,' he said, holding out his coffee cup to be refilled. 'I'll be home for lunch today. Please set it by the pool.'

'Oh, Fred,' said his wife. 'I shan't be here. I've got this wretched women's luncheon and I have to introduce the speaker.' This was not news to Fred Spillman. He had taken careful note when she first mentioned it three days earlier.

'Don't worry, dear, I've got a report to write. And I need to be away from the office to think straight.'

Spillman reached across for the small handbell next to his tumbler of whisky, and rang it, tingling with anticipation. Moments later Clarissa stepped through the open glass doors leading out from the lounge.

Fred Spillman watched her sway towards him and felt the desire pulse through his body. She stopped in front of him and he noticed the top button of her white housecoat was undone. He took hold of her long brown forearm and squeezed it gently.

'I want you now,' he said. 'Make sure all the doors are locked. I will close the lounge doors when I come in.'

'A few moments, master,' she smiled, 'and I will be ready for you.'

When he opened the bedroom door she was lying on the bed, naked, except for his wife's rings and gold bracelets on her hands; her white-gold and emerald necklace glittered around Clarissa's neck.

Fred Spillman moved across the room quickly and took her in his arms. The dusky scent of her body overpowered him.

Maddeningly the phone rang on the bedside table and

Fred Spillman snatched the receiver. 'Yes,' he said curtly, panting lightly.

'Fred,' yelled Mark Ashford, ' I've been ringing all over town for you. What the fuck are you doing at home?

Fred Spillman saw the fire flicker in Clarissa's eyes and for a moment, he was speechless.

19

Next day at the meeting, Eddie faced Fred Spillman for the first time. He felt distinctly uneasy at first, then David Maltby, with quiet tact and banking etiquette, introduced him as 'one of your largest shareholders who needs clarification on the Amanda deal'. And Eddie suddenly felt he had a legitimate reason to be there.

Spillman showed no trace of discomfort. He was charming. 'Be glad to help if I can,' he said showing Eddie to a chair at the polished, mahogany directors' table dominating the boardroom.

David Maltby sat down beside him, while Spillman, still smiling, sat across the table, flanked by two executives from the Amanda mine. At the far end of the table, Bill Borden, the big, affable, figurehead chairman of Eastern Mining, took a neutral seat at the end of the table.

'Do we stand – or should I say sit here – accused?' asked Fred Spillman genially.

'Not a bit of it Fred. There's an obvious misunderstanding and it's my duty as your banker to help clarify the situation.'

David Maltby outlined the situation with all the professional tact and diplomacy of a banker telling an important client he is being accused of fraud. There was no hint of any serious allegation and he spoke softly, his voice flat and matter of fact. When he mentioned the map and the borehole results Spillman nodded understandingly.

Eddie glanced across the table at Spillman. He was a short, squat, powerfully built man who reminded Eddie of a human terrier. His pink, flabby face was set firm and expressionless on his short, stout neck and his close-cropped hair was swept off his blunt forehead. He watched Spillman's piggy, light blue eyes darting from side to side missing little. Beneath the calm exterior, Fred Spillman struggled to contain his abundant energy. He moved his hands with quick decisive movements and when he blinked, he seemed to do it faster than anyone else. Small, puffy bags of tiredness hung beneath his eyes and he tapped the fingers of his right hand incessantly on the table as he spoke. If Fred Spillman had a tail, Eddie was sure it would wag permanently.

David Maltby passed the map and photos across the table.

'Take a look at these,' he told Spillman, who flicked through them, pausing a few moments at the map as his eyes darted around the borehole results.

At the far end of the table Bill Borden's mind switched off after a good lunch at the Rand Club. Had he been at his office, he would have had a nap on the sofa. Perhaps he could take one here. His eyes felt heavy and he wondered if he dare close them.

He lifted his eyelids slightly and focused hazily on the huddled meeting at the end of the table. They were too busy talking, they wouldn't even notice. He closed his eyes and he was asleep.

'Looks like Amanda,' Spillman said at last. He held up a photo. 'You can see our drilling rigs on this one.' Then he put his hand on his chest and smiled at David Maltby. 'And with all my heart David, I wish our results were as good as these. Unfortunately, they are not. The old workings are just like this, and we have been drilling in that area. But the figures . . .' He shook his head. 'They're not correct. I wish they were.'

'Here's the real story,' he said passing a file across the table. 'Our latest internal progress report. As you can see, the results and conclusions are very different from Mr Vandermeer's.' David Maltby took the report, read it, and handed it to Eddie.

'And that's all there is?' he asked Spillman.

'That is all there is,' replied Spillman, pronouncing each word slowly and emphatically. 'I understand why Mr Vandermeer wants to get the share price up – he's got a big block of shares.'

'So, for that matter, have you,' interupted Maltby. 'Well over thirty-five per cent.'

'Exactly. We would be delighted if he was right. But he's not. And that's all there is to it.'

A long, loud whine stopped the meeting and heads turned down the table to Bill Borden, head slumped forward, eyes closed. Wind had got the better of him in his sleep.

Eddie saw Fred Spillman's face tighten angrily.

'I'm sorry, David. He's retiring in a couple of months.'

David Maltby raised his eyebrows. 'What do you think Mr Vandermeer?'

'There's a big difference in the results,' said Eddie.

'Where did you get hold of that map?' Spillman asked Eddie.

'I can't tell you.' Eddie realized his mistake as soon as he had spoken.

Spillman seized his chance. 'In that case,' he said to David Maltby, 'I don't know how else I can help.' He picked up his report from the table, slid it into his briefcase and stood up. The two executives sprang to their feet either side of him.

'My advice to Mr Vandermeer,' said Spillman smiling at Eddie, 'is to ask whoever gave you the map to prove the figures.' He shrugged his shoulders. 'I'm afraid I can't.'

Spillman walked to the end of the table and shook Bill Borden's shoulder. 'We're off now, Bill,' he said. 'Don't bother to get up.' He shook hands with David Maltby, then Eddie, and closed the door firmly behind him.

Bill Borden woke up startled, his face puffed from sleep, his eyes bleary. He stretched his arms and yawned.

'Must have dropped off,' he said apologetically.

'Damn,' said David Maltby. 'I wanted Fred to leave me a copy of that report.'

'Shall I see if I can catch him?' offered Eddie.

'Which report?' asked Bill Borden eager to redeem himself.

'The drilling report on Amanda,' said Maltby.

'I've got one at the office. If you walk back with me, I'll give it to you.'

David Maltby glanced anxiously at his watch.

'It's OK. I'll pick it up,' Eddie said, 'and drop it off at your office.'

'Would you mind?'

'Not at all. It's on my way back to the market.'

20

'Nice chaps, those lads from Zimbabwe,' said Bill Borden as he unlocked a filing cabinet in his office and took out a pink file marked Eastern Mining. Eddie was lost for a reply. The men from Zimbabwe hadn't said a word the whole time. The man was a bigger fool than Eddie first thought.

'That must be it,' said Bill Borden triumphantly, plucking a report from the file and passing it to Eddie. 'Let me have it back in the morning. That's the original.'

Bill Borden had little to do with the day to day running of the business and had not read the report. Much of the paperwork that came into his office simply went through the filing system set up by his secretary.

Eddie opened the report and glanced at the first page. There must be a mistake, he thought. The words 'Private and Confidential – Chairman's office only' were typed across the top. Next to it was a handwritten message with a red ring round it. It said: 'Bill, please keep this somewhere safe.' It was signed 'Mark'. The report was headed: 'Prospects and drilling results for Amanda Gold Mine.'

Eddie looked through the first few pages. He hadn't read any of them before. After the first five pages, he came to the section he had read that afternoon. It was headed

'Drilling Results'. He glanced down at it and checked some of the gold grades. They were the same. Then he turned back to the first five pages of the report headed 'Prospects'. The last paragraph caught his eye.

In conclusion, it is my opinion that all these factors come together to make the old Amanda mine lease area one of the richest and most easily accessible deposits in Southern Africa. In sixteen years of working in the mines of South Africa and Zimbabwe I have not seen a mine that offers such scope and promise.

It was signed Ian Boysens, Mining Engineer, Eastern Mining.

They had been hoodwinked. Everything he and Izzie had found was true. He had to find David Maltby.

'Drink?' asked Bill Borden.

'Not for me thanks Bill.' He held up his watch and tapped the glass face. 'I'm late. My wife and I are leaving for Durban tomorrow and I promised my kids a barbecue.'

Minutes later he was in the elevator scanning through the report again. He knew he only had minutes if he was going to catch David Maltby at the office, but it was worth a try. The elevator bumped to a halt and he was on the street running the eight blocks to the Rand Reserve Bank head office. The streets were crowded with commuters and he made better time running on the side of the road than he did sidestepping the crowds on the pavement.

After four blocks he was panting hard but still running. He pulled the knot of his tie loose from his throat and opened the top two buttons of his shirt. He felt the sweat running down his temple now, but he did not slacken his pace. Once past the stock exchange, he knew he was almost there. He turned left into Rissik Street and there on the corner, two hundred yards in front of him stood the bank's headquarters.

He saw the black car waiting at the bottom of the steps, the chauffeur with the back door open, and David Maltby stepping smartly down the steps towards it.

He couldn't shout, there was something undignified

about screaming down the street at the chairman of the largest bank in the country, so he kept on running. As he closed to the last thirty yards, the black saloon pulled out onto Rissik Street and accelerated quietly away from him. He waved hoping the driver might see him in the rear mirror, but the car sped away from him. Further down Rissik Street the traffic lights turned from green to amber to red and Eddie Vandemeer stood there watching the chairman's car slow down. The lights were at the end of the block, a distance of about two hundred yards, where Rissik Street intersected with Main Street. He didn't hesitate. He was sprinting down Rissik Street well before the car stopped in front of the lights. He ran at full tilt, his lungs bursting, every muscle in his legs and arms hammering to their limit, and closed quickly on the stationary black saloon. The lights changed from red to amber, he heard the note of the engine rev higher as the driver prepared to move and then the lights were green. He was fifteen yards away, he might just make it. He summoned a final burst of energy, and sprinted the last few yards until he drew level with the back of the car.

'Stop! Stop!' he yelled. He slammed his fist down on to the roof of the car, then hammered repeatedly. The car slowed and an angry David Maltby lowered the electric window and peered out.

'What the hell are you doing? I thought we'd hit something.'

The front of Eddie's shirt was completely open and his tie hung over his shoulder. 'We've been tricked,' he panted. 'Here's the real report. Amanda's one of the richest deposits in Southern Africa.'

Eddie pulled the report from his jacket pocket and handed it through the car window.

'The first four pages weren't part of the report we saw this afternoon.' He was still panting from the run, streams of sweat ran down the side of his forehead. He straightened his tie, wiped his face with a handkerchief, and peered through the car window. David Maltby sat perched forward on the rear seat, his body taut with concentration, as he read.

'Where did you get this?' he asked.

'That idiot Bill Borden.'

When he finished Maltby shook his head in disbelief. 'The bastards,' he said, and opened the car door. 'Can I give you a lift back?'

'Thanks. I'll come back to your office and we can make a copy. I'm escaping tomorrow for a few days' holiday. Anything I can do?'

'No. Leave everything to me,' Maltby replied sternly. Eddie sat in the back recovering from the run.

The car turned round and sped back down Rissik Street while David Maltby dialled his private line number. It was answered on the second ring.

'Hilary, can you stay on for a while, something urgent has just come up.'

'Yes, of course.'

'Ring Fred Spillman. Find out where I can reach Mark Ashford. If you can't find Spillman, ring the South African Mining office in London or the headquarters in New York. I'll be with you in a couple of minutes.'

'Right, sir,' she replied.

'Well,' said Eddie, 'do you believe us now?'

'In twenty-five years of banking I've never seen anything like it,' he said sternly.

2 I

Mark Ashford woke suddenly. He lay in the dark listening for whatever had disturbed him, but there was nothing. Then he realised it wasn't a noise that had woken him. His sub-conscious had been working overtime. All evening, two interesting pieces of information from Max Llewellyn had gone round and round in his mind. First, Eddie Vandermeer had gone on holiday; second, he had borrowed nearly a million rand to buy his Eastern Mining stake.

Mark Ashford knew instinctively both events were significant and could be used to his advantage, but a plan eluded him. He glanced at the Rolex Oyster on his bedside table. Two o'clock. One o'clock in Johannesburg. His mind was too clear and sharp for sleep; some of his best financial manoeuvres had been planned in the quietness of the early morning.

He pulled on a silk dressing gown and walked down the deeply carpeted hallway to his study. He threw some logs on the heap of red embers in the fireplace, sat down on a sofa, and watched the flames dance in the darkened room. Outside, the night was still and the temperature below freezing. A heavy frost lay in long, white sweeps across the lawns around the house.

He dialled Max Llewellyn's home number in Johannesburg.

'Yes,' said a distant, sleepy voice.

'Max, I'm sorry to wake you up, but it's important.'

Mark heard Max fumble in the darkness and the phone clatter to the floor.

'Sorry.' His voice sounded more alert. 'Hang on – I'll take it downstairs.'

The line went dead, then the receiver was picked up again.

'Max, if the Eastern Mining price slumped where would it leave Vandermeer's loan?'

Max giggled slyly. 'If they couldn't come up with the difference between their assets and liabilities, you could kiss them goodbye.'

'Technically, the firm would be bankrupt, right?'

'Correct. And as such they would be "hammered" from the exchange.'

'Could they find the money?'

'I doubt it. But even if they did, the old man would have such a nasty shock he would probably make Eddie unwind his position.'

'Max, I own thirty-six per cent of Eastern Mining and I'll sell every share to get that price down. Can you make sure the auditors are at the door when it happens?'

'I could. As a council member I have a special responsibility on such matters. But . . . I'm not sure I should.'

Mark Ashford knew the approach. 'Your firm can handle all the sales and any repurchases. That's a lot of commission. We will have our usual agreement, same price as before, if you take charge of the dealing personally. I'll call Zurich and make the transfer.'

'When do you want me to start?'

'As soon as the market opens this morning.'

Izzie Van Royen's eyes narrowed when he saw Max Llewellyn bustling across the trading floor shortly after the exchange opened. Beneath the tight white shirt and grey mohair suit, Max's body bounded along with fresh vigour. In the next few days Max stood to make R100,000 personally, payable in Switzerland, and much more in commissions for his firm. And for that kind of money, he always gave his best.

There goes a man with a mission, thought Izzie, as Max passed him.

As stock-exchange president Max was a powerful member of the inner sanctum, who made the rules. He was also the greatest living expert on breaking them. And nothing quite turned Max on like walking that tightrope on the trading floor. At heart, he was a high-wire performer. He could dance, pirouette, and somersault. Max knew all the moves. There was only one dealer he had any respect for – Izzie Van Royen. When Izzie started to perform, Max usually got off the floor.

'Eastern Mining, seller,' yelled Max above the growing din and Izzie's head swung round.

He made two quick sales. 'Eastern Mining,' he called again and Izzie stepped over to him.

'You're making a lot of noise for a little man,' he said.

'Seller. Eastern Mining,' repeated Max quietly. Izzie saw the apprehension flicker in his baby-blue eyes.

'I know you're selling Max, I'm not a deaf fucking mute. What I want to know is who are you selling for?'

Max turned a diamond-studded gold ring uneasily round his centre finger.

'It's an institution. Don't like the stock.'

'I bet they don't. Who is it? The Trustees for the Blind School, the Johannesburg Sanatorium for the Terminally Insane? Or is it your friend Mark Ashford?'

'You know Mr Van Royen, you really should learn to treat members with at least the minimum of good manners. This is the floor of the Johannesburg stock exchange and I'm the president.'

'No, it's not,' shouted Izzie. 'It's a fucking whorehouse and you're no better than the resident pimp.'

Max started to speak and Izzie lifted his hand. 'Say one more word to me, and I'll smack you right in your fat, flabby little mouth.'

Max stared at him dumbfounded, his face gradually reddening with anger. The ridiculous part was, he knew Izzie meant it. He turned to go and Izzie grabbed his shoulder. 'And Max . . . don't forget,' he added threateningly, 'I'm watching every move you make.'

Izzie stood there smiling as he watched Max bounce away across the trading floor. He took a last long draw from his cigarette, stamped it out, and went over to his desk.

Throughout the morning he watched Max's outsize bald head, bobbing up and down at everyone else's shoulder height, as he weaved in and out of the traders on the floor. Max sold Eastern Mining steadily, and from time to time, was joined by some senior partner chums from other firms. Izzie knew the clique. All of them were sellers.

It was an old racket, Izzie had done the same many times before. At one stage, four dealing partners of the biggest firms were all selling. Their presence on the trading floor was a talking point in itself. But when they all started selling Eastern Mining, the price started to fall.

It started the morning at forty cents and slid steadily down to hit thirty-six cents by midday, where the price steadied up. A wave of selling flooded the market just before lunch, and Eastern Mining slumped to twenty-six cents 'offered'.

Max started the story in the members' bar before lunch

and it quickly spread to the bars and restaurants around Hollard Street. He had organized it well. By the time dealers were back in the market for the afternoon session, everyone knew South African Mining was off-loading its Eastern Mining stake in the market.

At the close of business, the price had fallen to twenty-two cents. The selling continued throughout the next day and on the morning of the third day, after another heavy bout of selling, Eastern Mining dropped to eighteen cents. The share price had more than halved in three trading sessions on a disclosed turnover of 350,000 shares. Izzie watched with fascination. Now the time had come for him to do a little 'huiswerk'.

22

A few minutes after the latest wave of selling died down, Max Llewellyn breezed into the general office. Deep inside his barrel chest he felt a twinge of excitement.

'Doug, pull out the latest quarterly returns from Vandermeer,' he told the clerk to the committee. 'There are rumours in the market about their finances.'

'Eastern Mining?' asked Doug Davies surprised.

'That's what I'm told,' replied Max sharply. He had a knack of banishing distasteful incidents in his life and had recovered from the confrontation with Izzie. Now he was back in a world where he was all powerful, his natural bumptiousness reflated.

Doug found the Vandermeer return and the pair studied it.

'Here we are,' said Max. 'Nine hundred thousand rand borrowed from Central Merchant Bank against Eddie Vandermeer's house and Eastern Mining shares.'

'What price are Eastern Mining?'

'They're dropping like there's no tomorrow. Some of the boys are talking them back to eleven cents.'

'So Vandermeer is insolvent?'

Max nodded. 'Afraid so. You'd better arrange for the auditors to go in. I'll call an emergency meeting of the committee.'

Armed with these figures, Max knew he would have little trouble convincing the others. When a firm the size of Vandermeer's went under, the other brokers picked up their clients.

William Vandermeer had broken a recent rule imposed by his surgeon after the last heart attack, and met an old friend from the market for lunch. Instead of the normal sandwich, glass of milk, and a leisurely walk round the shops he had consumed a large rib of beef and bottle of wine at Madame Sikorsky's. He felt comfortably full and the wine gave him a glowing sense of wellbeing as he stood checking through some prices on the screen.

But the sudden arrival of Peter Bancroft, the stock-exchange auditor, with a team of investigators, did nothing to help his digestion.

'Mr Vandermeer, I'm afraid it's your turn this week,' said Bancroft hesitantly. 'Just a routine check,' he added.

'Anything in particular?'

'No sir. You know how it is. Every now and then we check on member firms, and this time it's you.'

'I hope you're not going to make a song and dance about Eastern Mining? Come with me, I'll introduce you to our chief clerk.'

William Vandermeer led the small party to the general office where the firm's books and files were stored. Introductions were made, files were taken out and laid on desks around the office, and the investigation started.

'I'll leave you to it,' said William Vandermeer, still a little puzzled. 'I'll only get in your way. These people,' he pointed to two of his staff, 'know all there is to know. I'm only permitted in here on sufferance.' He smiled, and left.

Peter Bancroft went to work immediately. He had been told exactly what to look for and it wasn't many minutes before he found it.

Vandermeer & Vandermeer had borrowed R900,000 and placed the entire Eastern Mining holding with the bank as collateral. He worked out the average buying price. Although Eddie and Izzie had bought some cheap shares on the first raid, later purchases lifted their average price to thirty-one cents. If Eastern Mining stayed around its current price, Vandermeer & Vandermeer were exposed for about R400,000, a hefty shortfall for most people. Under stock-exchange rules, the difference had to be made up in cash, or near cash, like certificates of deposit or gilt-edged securities. Property was not allowed, for in a bad market it could prove difficult to sell.

Ten minutes after he arrived, Peter Bancroft phoned Llewellyn's meeting. The other committee members watched silently as Max made notes. He looked grave and his voice was stern, but Max was clearly enjoying himself.

'Bad news,' he said, when he had put down the phone. 'They've uncovered a deficit of R400,000. Vandermeer's are insolvent.'

He looked inquiringly at the other two committee members, both senior partners of big firms. 'I don't think we have much alternative do we?'

They shook their heads. William Vandermeer was one of the most respected men in the market and they were all loath to expel him. But the rules were clear and every broker should know them. Technically, Vandermeer & Vandermeer were bankrupt.

'Better we do it, than let the bank take control,' said Max. 'If it's any worse, at least we could contain the publicity.'

The other two men nodded their agreement.

He dialled Vandermeer & Vandermeer's number and waited to be put through to the stock-exchange auditor. As he waited, he twiddled the gold ring round his plump, middle finger.

'Peter, we've talked about this,' he told Bancroft. 'Vandermeer's may have to be hammered. Give them a chance to come up with the cash, but we can't afford to wait. If we don't move, the bank will.'

'Leave it to me. Did you know Eddie is away?'

'That's not our problem. It wouldn't change the situation if he was here. Either the family's got the money or they haven't. It's cash or they're out.'

William Vandermeer was sitting at his desk writing when Peter Bancroft returned. He pointed to one of two red leather chairs. 'Sit down, Peter'.

'Your loan from Central is bad news, I'm afraid, Mr Vandermeer.'

'The bank are well secured.'

'Rule 163 says your assets must exceed your liabilities at all times.'

'I know that.'

'Eastern Mining's share price slumped, yesterday and the day before. Did you see it?'

William Vandermeer nodded. 'We know Eastern Mining and we know the potential of the Amanda. The decline is a short-term fluctuation. Once the company finishes its drilling tests, I'm sure there will be a favourable announcement.'

'But the point is, Mr Vandermeer, with the share price at nineteen cents, your firm is trading with a R400,000 deficit.'

'The price has dropped that much?' William Vandermeer was incredulous.

'Absolutely. Eastern Mining have halved in the last three days. Your R900,000 loan is now secured by under R500,000 worth of shares.'

'Are you saying we're finished?' demanded the old man. He stood up behind his desk, his frail body taut, his eyes glaring angrily.

'Unless you can come up with the shortfall in cash, Vandermeer's is insolvent.'

'Now wait a minute,' said Vandermeer. 'The share price has only been down two days. It could bounce back tomorrow – or certainly when the company makes a statement about its drilling results.'

'It might – or it might drop another fifty per cent. Rules are rules I'm afraid.'

For William Vandermeer the conversation was dreamlike, not really happening. He was an observer. Then the old fire returned, and his hands shook slightly from anger.

'Are you telling me we're hammered?'

'I'm afraid I am.'

'Rules are one thing, but we're talking about people's jobs, their families, their futures. Not to mention the clients.'

Peter Bancroft was not enjoying this. Over the years he had performed the same unpleasant task with a handful of brokers, but somehow they were different. Most of them were rogues, who knew they had broken the rules in one form or another and showed few signs of remorse when found out. But this was different. No crime had been committed.

'Look, there is one way out.' he said. 'Can you make up the R400,000 shortfall in cash?'

'Where the hell from? I have assets – the house, shares, but nothing like that.'

'You would have to give the committee an assurance today that the money would be forthcoming immediately.'

'Out of the question. I might be able to raise some through friends. My son Eddie has some money, but I can't reach him at the moment. He's out of touch.'

Bancroft stared at his shoes.

'Have you spoken to the finance committee about this?'

'They know I'm here. There's not one of the committee who would want my job right now. They're all very sorry.'

'I bet they are,' retorted William Vandermeer. 'Can't wait to divide up my clients.'

Bancroft shrugged. 'I don't think anyone wishes you harm. But obviously no committee can afford to ignore the situation. Particularly with a business your size.'

William Vandermeer could not believe it. His mind spun. The business, his security, his reputation in the financial community, were all threatened. He would have to summon all the guile of his early years to save the situation. But each time he came to the same conclusion – there was no way he could find R400,000.

Suddenly William Vandermeer felt breathless. A spasm of pain ripped through the centre of his chest. He slumped forward onto his desk gasping, the pain closing an iron fist around his rib cage.

Bancroft rushed over to him as the old man fumbled in his jacket pocket for his heart pills. He got the bottle open and a stream of white pills cascaded onto the desk top. But it was too late.

There was a space when all he felt was pain – then he knew he couldn't endure it any longer.

Six minutes later William Vandermeer was fighting for his life under a white plastic oxygen tent in the intensive care unit at Johannesburg's Central Hospital.

At 3.30 pm that afternoon, the trading bell rang out dolefully and the handful of brokers chatting in the market turned to hear the announcement. Vandermeer & Vandermeer were ceremoniously 'hammered'.

23

Eddie pulled hard on the rudder and felt the round, white wood beam of the sloop swirl beneath him in the deep blue Indian Ocean. When the jib swung round, he tightened the mainsail ropes and, sailing close to wind, headed out through the foaming surf.

A strong breeze ballooned the tall, navy mainsail, and he felt the sloop surge forward. The salty sea spray stung his skin as the crashing bows rose and fell through the waves. The sails gave short sharp cracks when they moved off the wind, and each time Eddie pulled the rudder back into line.

The sun burnt down through the breeze and Eddie felt it on his shoulders. The wind smelt thick with salt and he could taste it on his lips. The new course took them away from the coastline towards the horizon and into the full glare of the midday sun.

'What the hell are you doing?' yelled Lucy. 'You nearly

rolled me into the sea.' She lay naked on her back on the curved white roof of the sloop's cabin, clutching on to the wooden handrails either side of the roof, her long black hair streaming back in the wind.

Eddie locked the rudder into self-steering and moved quickly along the side of the boat, his feet hardly touching the glistening deck to avoid the heat.

He stood over her, his shadow blocking the sun on her face and she opened her eyes. He leant over and kissed her. A sudden high wave made the boat fall then lurch to one side and Eddie struggled to regain his balance. Lucy's hand grabbed his arm and pulled him towards her.

'You can't leave me now,' she laughed, 'it was just getting interesting.'

He grasped the mast with one hand to steady himself.

'Hold on tight,' she said, her arms firmly round him. 'If you go, I go with you.'

They kissed and their bodies clung together.

'Not here,' said Lucy slightly out of breath. 'Come with me.'

Half an hour later, Eddie slipped out of the double bunk in the small main cabin and made his way up to the cockpit to check the position of the boat. He scanned the horizon. That was lucky, he thought, no other boats around.

He unhooked the rudder from the self-steering gear, and set a fresh course straight up the coast. Below deck he heard the clatter of plates as Lucy prepared lunch.

They had sailed from Lucy's parents' house two days earlier, headed for the Blue Lagoon hotel, some forty miles up the coast. The house was built into the cliffs facing the sea with spectacular views. It was midsummer in Natal, long, hot days that smouldered through to late evening. They played tennis for hours on the clay court in the garden, swam in the strong Natal surf, and went for long walks along the deserted white sand beach.

In the afternoon, they slept under the half-covered patio, away from the powerful glare of the sun. Evenings, they went to the beach for a swim, then barbecued supper at a favourite outcrop of flat rocks while the sun set in a blistering explosion of pink and red behind the rolling green hills of sugar cane.

But the sailing trip was the highlight of the week. Eddie had learnt to sail in Cape Town around the turbulent waters of the Cape of Good Hope and ocean sailing had always been part of his life. He only knew how much he missed it when he was back on a boat.

'Take these for me, Eddie,' called Lucy from the galley and stood on the steps holding two plates of tuna, salad, asparagus and tomatoes. He took the plates and she followed him, carrying two glasses and a bottle of cold white wine.

They ate lunch and drank the wine, balancing plates and glasses precariously against the pitch. When they finished, Lucy rolled sideways and lay across Eddie's lap. She rested her head on the bow of the boat and rubbed the back of his neck.

'Glad we came?' she asked. He stroked the wisps of long black hair off her face and kissed her.

'Hating it,' he smiled.

The swell calmed, but the breeze stayed strong and Eddie changed course again to make better speed. Two hours later the Blue Lagoon hotel was in sight, and he and Lucy started to pull down the sails. The hotel was built on the beach at the head of a small bay tucked into the rocky coastline. It was a naturally sheltered spot with high cliffs rising either side of the narrow inlet entrance. The hotel resembled a game lodge with flat pampas-grass roofs and steps up to a large balcony. A figure appeared on the balcony as Eddie steered the boat towards a makeshift jetty in front of the hotel. As soon as the sloop was alongside, a man came running down.

'Mr Vandermeer?'

'Yes.'

'I'm the manager of the hotel. We've been expecting you. Your mother has called several times. So has a Mr Van Royen. Your father has had a heart attack. He's in hospital.'

'How is he? Is he all right?'

'Your mother says he's stabilized. If you'd like to use the house phone . . .'

Eddie turned to Lucy. 'Looks like we're going home in a hurry, darling. Will you pack?'

'Of course. I'll see you inside.'

Eddie ran into the hotel and dialled his mother. There was no reply, so he rang Izzie.

'Christ man, where the hell have you been? I've been trying to reach you for the past two days.'

'Are we still talking?'

'Don't be a fool,' snapped Izzie. 'Look, Mark Ashford and his cronies have really got you this time. You've been hammered.'

'That's crazy. How can they do that?'

'They've done it. It nearly killed your father. He's had another heart attack.'

'How bad is he?'

'OK at the moment. But I shouldn't hang around if I were you. I'll give you all the details when you get here. And, Eddie, I'm sorry.'

24

Jan Smuts airport
Johannesburg
5.30p.m.

Izzie Van Royen stood outside on the first-floor observation platform at Jan Smuts airport and watched the South African Airways' blue and gold Boeing screech down the runway through the early stillness of a Johannesburg summer evening. He checked his watch; the plane was fifteen minutes late. He walked inside to the bar, ordered a beer and drank it slowly at the bar while the 747 taxied round to the front of the terminal. Passengers streamed down the stairways, but Izzie didn't see Eddie and Lucy immediately.

There were no customs checks on internal flights, so he finished his drink and went down to the arrival exit. Eddie and Lucy were first out, pushing trolleys loaded with brown leather cases, flight bags, and presents for the children.

'Good to see you, pal,' said Eddie, stretching out his hand.

'You too, boy.' Lucy left her trolley, gave Izzie a short hug and a kiss on the cheek.

'How is he?' asked Eddie.

'No better, no worse. I promised your mother I'd take you straight to the hospital – she's at home with your kids. He's been unconscious most of the time, but whenever he comes round he asks for you. I've got your car outside.'

'I'll drop you two off at the hospital and take the car back to the house,' said Lucy. 'The children will be worried and I can be with your mother.'

Minutes later Lucy drove them down the empty freeway for the short ride to the hospital.

'So what the hell's going on?' asked Eddie.

'It's Llewellyn and his cronies,' said Izzie. 'It rained Eastern Mining shares for three days. When the market operation was complete they sent the auditors in.'

'And Mark Ashford?' added Eddie. 'No one else owns enough shares to bombard the price like that.'

Izzie lit a cigarette and inhaled deeply. 'He's the bastard behind it.'

'When did you hear?'

'Just after it happened. I saw Max selling the shares in the market but I had no idea at the time . . .' He left the sentence unfinished as Lucy turned the car into the main entrance of the hospital.

'I'll see you later, darling,' said Lucy. 'Give my love to your father.'

They signed in at the visitor's desk then Izzie led Eddie up to the third-floor intensive-care unit. A nurse met them from the elevator and took them to William Vandermeer's room.

'I'm afraid he's very weak,' she said to Eddie.

'Will he be all right?'

'We hope so,' she smiled and carefully opened the door.

William Vandermeer lay on a high steel hospital bed, propped up by starchy white pillows. A white plastic tent hung from the ceiling and surrounded the bed. He wore blue and white striped hospital pyjamas, for there had been no time to get his own. Later, the doctors dared not move him.

Eddie looked at his father in dismay. He had seen him after heart attacks twice before, but never looking quite so ill or pathetic. His skin was grey against the white of his hair and the spiky white stubble on his face, and his head lay heavily on one side of his pillow as he slept. Drip-feed tubes hung down inside the tent and were attached to the insides of his wrists. A black mask covered his mouth and from the rhythm of his breathing Eddie guessed it was attached to a machine beside the bed. As his father breathed out, the machine breathed in.

Eddie felt a wave of remorse. If he hadn't got involved with Eastern Mining in the first place, or the loan from the bank, this would never have happened. He swore to himself he would never ever gamble like this again. He loved the excitement of taking risks, but this was too much. This had not been part of his calculations. This he had no stomach for.

The room was quiet except for the gasping of the oxygen machine and the quiet hiss of the air conditioning. Eddie walked across the room and sat down beside the bed. The nurse checked the dials on the machines and left the room. Izzie remained a few steps back from the end of the bed, his head slightly bowed.

Now he was closer, Eddie saw more tubes going into the centre of his father's chest to one side of the heart. The plastic tent hung loosely over the bed and Eddie pulled one side out a little, slipped an arm inside the tent and held his father's hand. It felt warm, and he stroked the back of it gently with the side of his thumb. Lightly he held his wrist and felt the weak beat of the old man's pulse.

William Vandermeer slowly swung his head from one side of the pillow to the other and opened his eyes. He focused on nothing for a moment, his eyes still dazed from drugs. Then he showed signs of drowsy recognition. His gaze fell first to Eddie's hand; he lifted his head and smiled when he saw his son. Eddie saw the twinkle return to his father's eyes.

'Dad, I'm sorry . . .' William Vandermeer lowered his eyelids slowly and shook his head. He squeezed his son's hand. He could not speak but he wanted to tell Eddie not to worry.

The nurse came back into the room and William Vandermeer pointed to his mask. She understood and drew back the side of the plastic tent on Eddie's side of the bed.

'Not for too long, Mr Vandermeer,' she said. 'We don't want you getting tired.'

She carefully lifted the mask from William Vandermeer's face and Eddie bent closer.

The old man spoke in a hoarse whisper, the words coming slowly. 'Eddie, you mustn't blame yourself. Mark Ashford set us up. It was my fault as much as yours.' He squeezed Eddie's hand again and smiled, his eyes lighting up with that old warmth. 'I must rest now,' he whispered and slowly he faded back to sleep, still clasping Eddie's hand.

The nurse returned and replaced the oxygen mask. Moments later William Vandermeer was asleep, the sound of his breathing lifting and falling quietly with the gasps of the oxygen machine.

'Let him sleep now,' said the nurse. 'We can give you a bed if you would like to stay?'

'Thank you.' He turned to Izzie. 'Would you call in on my mother. Tell her I'm staying with Dad tonight. I'll call Lucy.'

'Sure. I'll be back with an overnight bag for you.'

The flight from Durban and the shock of seeing his father had drained Eddie. He fell asleep moments after his head sunk into the pillow and the crisp white hospital sheets and blankets were drawn over his shoulders.

The hand of the nurse shook him awake four hours later. 'Mr Vandermeer, Mr Vandermeer, come quickly, please.'

He woke instantly, dressed, still half asleep, and ran down the hospital corridor, doing up his shirt. As he approached, a doctor walked out of the room.

'Mr Vandermeer?'

'Yes.'

'I'm sorry. Your father is dead. He had a massive heart attack. There was nothing we could do.'

Eddie felt the rage boil in his body. Streams of tears burnt down his cheeks. 'Mark Ashford,' he swore to himself, 'I'll get you for this.'

25

The flight from Johannesburg to New York was long and tiring and gave Eddie his first real chance to think through events since his father's death three weeks earlier. There was little he could do at home – the stock exchange had taken over the winding up of the firm – and once the family had settled down, Eddie decided to get out of South Africa for a while.

Lucy suggested it. She transferred R50,000 of her own money to a separate account for Eddie and said she would hold the fort at home. Izzie settled it.

'Do some *huiswerk*, man. Find him, track him down and kick the shit out of him.' The words were inimitably Izzie's, but Eddie knew what he meant. His life had been wrecked by someone he had never met, someone he had never seen. He had to confront the man. New York, the headquarters of Mark Ashford's mining empire, was as good a place as any to start.

The plane was half full and he sat at the back with an empty seat either side of him. Airline meals came and went, so did the drinks trolley, and every few hours he stretched out across the seats and dozed. Most times he dreamt about his father. He sat in bed talking to Eddie, telling him not to worry. He would soon be well and out of hospital, like last time. Each time Eddie woke there was that same frightening confusion. Was he really dead? The repeated shock of never seeing his father again was the cruellest trick of all.

But for Eddie's mother it was much worse. A small, frail, lady, warm and charming with a wonderful sense of fun, she had remained strong until the last. Although she knew her husband was dead, she hadn't really faced what his death meant. She busied herself making arrangements for the cremation, packing his clothes – doing things for him as she had always done.

She stood throughout the short memorial service in the crematorium chapel, quiet and composed, dressed in a black silk suit, a lace shawl over her head and shoulders. She was solitary and broken-hearted, apart for the first time from the man with whom she had spent her life.

In front of her, William Vandermeer lay in a polished pine coffin. Two middle-aged pall-bearers stood either side of it in shiny morning suits. One had curly black hair, heavily oiled, and dandruff across his shoulders. A panel in the wall slid back and to the sound of canned classical music she watched the coffin move towards the opening on a slow, noiseless conveyor. And then William Vandermeer was gone forever.

She turned to Eddie. He saw the tears welling up in her eyes, the look of devastation on her face. She bit her lip lightly to help keep control. But the tears streamed down her face. Eddie took her thin body into his arms, and could do nothing to stop her sudden, uncontrollable sobbing.

Eddie wasn't a violent man. But something had changed in him these last two weeks, and left him with one burning resolve – to hunt down and get even with Mark Ashford. It was a debt of honour. And he was determined William Vandermeer was going to be paid in full.

As soon as he was clear of the landing procedures at John F. Kennedy airport, Eddie took a cab to his old friend, Pierre Bouchard, head of the bullion-dealing room at Federal Union. He hadn't seen Pierre for nearly two years, though he had spoken to him many times on the phone.

Pierre's operation hadn't changed since the last time Eddie was in New York, two years earlier. There was that same sense of pulsating excitement around the bank of desks in the dealing room, the phones and flashing switchboards, as terse, gaunt-faced young dealers traded gold in massive amounts around the world's financial centres.

And Pierre was as charming as ever. His soft French accent seemed strangely out of place amongst all those New York drawls.

'Good to see you again, Eddie.' He shook his hand warmly and clasped his shoulder. 'I can't tell you how sorry I am about your father and the business . . .'

'Thanks. It's been a bad time all round.'

'Some coffee? A drink? I'm afraid I can't get away for lunch. The gold market is going mad. The price jumped eight dollars this morning.'

'Really?' asked Eddie mildly surprised. It seemed an age since he'd thought about the gold price.

'The Arabs are buying, and there are some big orders coming through the central American banks.'

A phone rang on Pierre's desk. '*Cherie* – I said no calls.' Then he paused. 'Tell him I'll call back.'

A dealer knocked at the door. 'Pierre, the Swiss are coming in strong buyers.'

'Why?' laughed Pierre. 'It's the middle of the night in Zurich.'

'I don't know. The price has jumped another three dollars.'

'You know the Swiss,' grinned Eddie. 'They never sleep when there's money to be made. I can see you're going to be busy. We'll meet later.'

'Where are you staying?'

'Nowhere yet.'

'*Parfait*,' said Pierre. He handed Eddie a key with a leather address tag on it. 'The key to my apartment. Make yourself at home. I'll be back as soon as I can. Chantelle's away for the week in Paris seeing her family. It's Friday – we'll go up to the chalet and do some skiing.'

'I'd love to stay Pierre, but I'm not sure about the skiing. I'm really not in the mood.'

Pierre put his arm round Eddie's shoulder. 'Be good for you,' he said. 'A complete change of scene.'

Eddie came over the hump at the top of the main run at high speed, crouched low on his skis and soared into the crisp mountain air. The wind rushed in his ears as he flew, his body tightly bunched, skis clamped together. He saw the ski runs and valley stretch out far below him. He felt exhilarated and full of energy.

Then he started to fall. He hit the icy slope with a light thump, quicker and harder than he should, his legs just mistiming the impact. He hurtled forward out of control, straight down the run. He slammed his right pole into the light-packed snow, swung hard on it for a split second and veered off on a wide sweep across the face of the slope towards a run down through the trees.

Pierre drew alongside. 'That was close,' he yelled laughing. 'Last one down buys lunch. And dinner.'

Four times that day they skied down from the top. As dusk fell, and the lights of the ski station flickered on, they unclipped their skis for the last time, their bodies tired and aching.

'Come on, I'll buy you a beer,' said Eddie.

'I've got a better idea. Let's go to the hot springs.'

'Where?'

'The hot springs,' repeated Pierre. 'They're a mile down the road. Takes all the ache out of your muscles. We'll pick up some wine and a couple of towels.'

They drove first to the chalet then down the precipitously winding road to the bottom of the valley and turned off along a track. Pierre stopped the car and they climbed over a gate, tramped through thick, crisp snow across a field, then climbed down the side of a deep gorge.

'Are you sure this is a good idea?' said Eddie.

'Courage, *mon vieux*,' replied Pierre. 'All will soon be revealed.'

Although it was dark, the sky was clear and bright and the whiteness of the snow outlined the landscape. The valley was narrow with steep sides, the river winding through the middle. It flowed down from the high snow fields above the ski resort, its icy waters swollen by melted snow. Twisting and falling through the steep, wooded, mountain slopes, it cascaded down a sharp escarpment into the head of the gorge, a foaming blue and white torrent.

The torrent became a swell as the river widened out across the scrubland floor and by the time it reached a turn in the middle of the valley, the water had calmed to a fast-moving flow.

'Not much further,' said Pierre. Eddie grunted. Just past the bend in the river and sheltered by an arm of boulders that stretched out into the current, the water was calm and the bank was shallow, flat and sandy. Hot springs bubbled up through the sand, giving off a slightly sulphorous odour.

Eddie wrinkled his nose, as he pulled off his clothes. 'I hope this feels nicer than it smells,' he said.

Although the water was sheltered around the hot springs, it grew deeper and colder further out into the river, and the opposite bank was deeply rutted from the swirling current.

They found a shallow place and gently stretched out in the surprising warmth. Pierre unscrewed the wine and took a swig. He twirled the cap back on, dropped the bottle into the water and watched it float downstream to Eddie.

'And now, *mon ami*, time for a straight question. You've been quizzing me all day about him. Whatever we talk about you swing the conversation round to Mark Ashford and South African Mining. Level with me. If I can help, I will.'

For the next fifteen minutes, Eddie sat in the warm bubbling waters, surrounded by snow on the river banks, and related the story of his visit to Amanda with Izzie, and his subsequent share purchases.

Pierre listened intently.

'Are you sure Mark Ashford is behind it all?'

'Absolutely.'

'You know he's a client?'

'What?' said Eddie surprised. 'You've never mentioned it.'

'It would be difficult for him not to be. Federal Union is one of the biggest gold traders in New York. Mark Ashford is one of the biggest producers. We're in the middle of negotiating a new contract to double his gold production in Zimbabwe.'

Eddie thought for a moment. 'Pierre, would you give me a copy of that contract? I could blow Mark Ashford to pieces.'

'And where does that leave me? Ever hear of client confidentiality? There's two people in my bank who know – me and my chairman.'

'I won't tell a soul,' said Eddie.

'Not yet,' said Pierre emphatically. 'Perhaps once it's signed and circulated round other departments. Maybe – and I mean maybe . . . I admired your father very much. And this whole business really stinks.'

'How long?'

The moon came over the hill and lit up the place like a spotlight. 'Eddie, I don't know. Two months, three months, perhaps longer. If I can I will, but you mustn't rely on it. I'll do my best, I promise.'

'If my father means anything to you, get me a copy of that contract.'

Pierre could see Eddie's face clearly now through the steam.

'You're really going to take him on, aren't you?' he said mildly surprised.

'I just hope I get the chance.'

26

A combination of two days skiing and jetlag had taken its
toll. As soon as they returned from the mountains, Eddie
went to bed exhausted and slept for fourteen hours. He still
felt tired the next morning as he stumbled round Pierre's
kitchen, unshaven and drowsy in a borrowed dressing
gown, looking for filter papers to make coffee.

There was no sign of Pierre so Eddie presumed he had
gone to work. Then he found a note. 'If you wake up in
time, how about lunch? Come to the office at 1.00 p.m.' It
was signed 'P'. The note stood on top of a packet of filter
papers.

Eddie made a jug of coffee, picked up the *New York Times*
business section from the kitchen table and retired to the
lounge sofa. He was halfway through the market report
when the front door bell buzzed.

David Maltby stood in the doorway. He wore a double
breasted, grey and white pinstripe suit, sported a red carn-
ation in his buttonhole, and had a triumphant twinkle in
his eye.

'I phoned your wife in Johannesburg,' he smiled, 'and
after the third degree she gave me this address. May I
come in?'

'Of course.' Eddie felt embarrassed at not being dressed.
'Excuse the attire. I wasn't expecting visitors.'

David Maltby waved the apology aside. 'I'm not staying,
but I wanted to see you.'

He refused coffee and sat down in the lounge facing
Eddie.

'I'm sorry about your father and the business. It seemed
everything happened at once.'

'It was no accident,' thought Eddie, but said nothing. David Maltby was still Mark Ashford's banker.

'After lengthy inquiries about the report you gave me, my bank has reached certain conclusions. I've come to put these to Mark Ashford at his office this morning, then I'm flying back to Johannesburg. I know it's been a terrible time for you and I wanted to thank you personally. Your efforts may not have helped you much, but you did my bank a great service.'

'What are you going to tell Ashford?' asked Eddie.

'I can't say precisely. That's between banker and client. But I wouldn't have made the trip if it wasn't very serious indeed.'

David Maltby stood up. 'My best wishes to my dear friend Mr Van Royen when you next see him,' he said jauntily as he walked towards the door. 'And thank you again.'

Once he had gone, Eddie walked back into the lounge and dialled the code for Johannesburg. 'If the balloon is going up,' thought Eddie, 'Izzie should know about it.'

'Izzie?'

'Yes.'

'David Maltby's just turned up. Sounds as if he's over here to present Ashford with an ultimatum.'

'Like what?'

'He wouldn't say – client confidentiality. But I got the clear impression he was here to put the boot in.'

'Good. Maybe we should do the same.'

Johannesburg
Tuesday, 1.00 p.m.

Even in civilian casual clothes, Captain Hendrik Viljoen, the Afrikaans head of the Johannesburg Fraud Squad at John Vorster Square, had the appearance of a police chief. He sat across the lunch table from Izzie at Madame Sikorsky's, his back straight in his chair, his blue cotton shirt sharply creased down each arm.

If South Africa had a Hitler youth, Captain Viljoen would have been an ideal candidate to lead it. His hair was close cropped and blond and his thin angular face had bright blue sunken eyes that missed nothing. And he looked quite the part in the knee-length black boots and tightly pressed jodhpurs.

Izzie had not seen Captain Viljoen for some months and the talk centred on their past exploits as they worked through their first course. Izzie noticed how the captain used his knife and fork with almost military precision as he sliced his way through a plate of smoked salmon.

The pair sat at Izzie's favourite corner table. From here he could take careful note of which dealers lunched together, without being immediately obvious himself.

Madame Sikorsky's was the market restaurant, a safe haven of good food and simple décor for professional punters. Madam Sikorsky knew them all, and her favourites she called by their Christian names. She was round and effervescent and spent the hectic lunch hour moving from table to table, and checking orders in the kitchen. She laughed and joked as she went but had an unerring sense of when clients wanted to be left alone.

And so it was this lunchtime with Izzie and his guest. She wasn't sure if she particularly welcomed Captain Viljoen among her clientele, but she could tell Izzie didn't want to be interrupted. The two sat huddled over the table while the waiter cleared away their first-course plates, and another wheeled in a trolley of steaming hot spare ribs, spaghetti and meatballs, both house 'specials' in constant demand.

Izzie lifted his glass to the captain. '*Meneer*, it is good to see you again.'

'You too, Izzie.'

They clinked glasses.

'Well,' said the captain with a smile, 'we never meet like his over lunch without a reason. What is it?'

'*Mein* captain,' said Izzie, putting down his glass. 'You may have read in the newspapers, particularly the English press, that South African Mining is proposing to sell off one of its subsidiaries.'

'Hasn't there been a lot of trading in the shares because they think there's been a new discovery?' Captain Viljoen didn't miss much.

'That's the one. I'm involved with a friend of mine, Eddie Vandermeer. We own twenty per cent of the company.'

'And someone's trying to steal it from you?' asked Captain Viljoen with a smile. 'Who are the mysterious Swiss buyers?'

'No prizes for guessing, captain.'

'Ashford?'

'No question about it,' said Izzie.

'You're absolutely sure?'

'Captain, we have tackled similar situations in the past and I think each time you have found my information correct.'

'Impeccable.' Captain Viljoen lifted his glass. 'Delicious,' he said. 'What do you want me to do about Eastern Mining?'

'Wait for the word – then bust it wide open.'

27

It was seven-thirty next day and Izzie sat on the small side patio of his house in the early morning sun, drinking his first coffee of the day and flipping through the *Rand Daily Mail*. He saw the story as soon as he turned to the finance section, stretched across the page as main lead.

SOUTH AFRICAN MINING DROPS AMANDA DEAL

The controversial plan by South African Mining to sell it Amanda lease areas as grazing land has been shelved for th time being so that the company can complete and possibly exten an exploratory drilling operation in progress for some months.

This will come as a welcome relief to minority shareholders i

Eastern Mining, which owns the Amanda mine, who believe a new mining prospect could be re-opened.

Izzie skipped through the rest of the story. So this was how they were going to get out of it, a simple withdrawal. He picked up the telephone.

'Have you seen the paper, captain?'

'I'm reading it now,' replied Captain Viljoen, tersely. 'Looks like you were right.'

'Has my information ever been wrong?'

The captain laughed quietly. 'Not yet. But there's always a first time.'

'Can you move on them now?'

'Don't worry, *Meneer*. Leave everything to me. I'll pick you up in half an hour.'

When it came to tracking down and exposing fraud, Captain Viljoen pursued his prey relentlessly. He planned his police operations with military precision learnt in the secret-service section of the South African army and, like many policemen, had a clear-cut simple definition of right and wrong.

At 8.35 a.m., Jack Plane drove into the basement garage of South African Mining's Johannesburg headquarters, having been secretly tailed from his house by an unmarked South African Police squad car.

Shortly after Plane arrived, three more police cars pulled up. Captain Hendrik Viljoen sat in the front seat of the first car, taut with excitement. South African Mining was one of the big five mining companies in South Africa, which made the job important enough. But it was English owned and operated. To catch an English mining house red-handed would almost certainly ensure promotion from his Afrikaner bosses.

He unclipped the intercom from the dashboard. 'All right, men, After me, no mistakes. Seize every file, no one must leave the building. And that means no one.'

He turned to Izzie Van Royen in the back seat. 'Where are these press men you tipped off?'

'Over there,' said Izzie, pointing to a blue Chevrolet parked across the street.

Viljoen turned to the driver. 'OK. Take the rear of the building. There's only a fire escape, but you never know. Izzie, you stay here.'

Captain Viljoen sprang out of the car and dashed up the steps, followed by a handful of officers. He barged through the swing doors into the entrance hall.

'Where's Jack Plane?' shouted Viljoen at a black security guard, shoving him to one side.

'Ten,' replied the amazed guard, watching them run towards the lifts.'

He snatched up the internal phone on the wall behind him and dialled.

'Police on their way up, master. They wouldn't stop. Plenty of them.'

The line went dead as Jack Plane slammed down the phone. He didn't need to be told twice. The offices were being raided. He pulled out the keys to the safe and filing cabinet and unlocked both. He bundled some files into a leather briefcase and opened the French doors onto the roof garden.

As he stepped out, the door burst open and Captain Viljoen and his men ran into the office. Plane's spindly body bolted across the patio, and up the black metal fire escape to a flat warehouse roof behind the South African Mining building.

'He's mine,' yelled Captain Viljoen running after him.

Plane surprised himself with his nimbleness and speed. Although he was never far from a drink, he rarely over ate, and his long thin frame had unexpected agility. He tore down the fire escape on the other side of the warehouse and then up a side lane into Hollard Street. As he turned the corner into Hollard Street he swung round and saw the uniformed figure of Captain Viljoen running across the warehouse roof.

He had to get his passport and money from his room a

the Carlton hotel, some distance away. Without it he couldn't get out of the country – officially, or unofficially through one of the neighbouring states. And that was all Jack Plane wanted to do. It was one thing for a local director to be arrested, but for the finance director of an international mining house the size of SAM to be locked up was quite another story.

He ran down Hollard Street as fast as he could, passing the stock exchange on his right. At the first set of traffic lights he spotted an empty taxi waiting for the lights to change and jumped into the rear seat.

'Carlton hotel, fast as you can,' he shouted at the driver, panting hard.

As the taxi pulled away he turned round to see Captain Viljoen running down Hollard Street behind him. For a while he was safe.

The taxi deposited him outside the main entrance to the Carlton hotel and he ran up to his second-floor room without waiting for the lift. He grabbed his passport and ten thousand dollars in assorted currencies from a locked cabinet and left. He dashed down the escalator stairway into the foyer and turned towards the big glass doors at the hotel's main entrance just as Captain Viljoen burst through them.

There was a split second as both parties froze, then Jack Plane ran back up the escalator steps and just made it through the closing doors of the elevator. He pressed the button for the twentieth floor. Each time he passed a floor he pressed its 'stop' button to confuse the captain and give the elevator a slow return ride.

He sprang out at the top floor gripping the briefcase tightly and ran up a flight of stairs to the roof-garden restaurant, set around a large kidney-shaped pool. The views across Johannesburg were fabulous and it was a favourite haunt among the business community for lunch. But its special appeal for Jack Plane was that it had a staff elevator that went down to the ground-floor kitchens. And he gambled that Viljoen might not know this.

He pushed his way through the crowded tables to the

pool in the middle of the restaurant, and walked hurriedly towards the serving exit.

'Stop that man,' bellowed Captain Viljoen as he charged into the restaurant, silencing the clatter and din of cutlery and conversation instantly. He ran straight for Plane, pushing waiters, food trolleys and customers out of his way.

Jack Plane stood on the edge of the pool, his way round blocked by a couple at a table and a waiter wheeling a trolley of soup terrines. He would have to jump from one edge of the pool to the other. He half turned to see the police captain flying through the air towards him, arms outstretched. As he jumped, his knees locked mid-flight as Viljoen's arms clamped around him in a mid-air tackle. The flying weight of the captain's body sent him crashing into the water in a gigantic belly flop that soaked every table and customer down one side of the pool. Viljoen hit the water seconds later, dragging a trolley of tomato soup terrines, a waiter, and a table of roast meats in after him. By the time Jack Plane surfaced the place had exploded in uproar.

The pool was ringed with guests staring down at him in disbelief. He stood in tomato-soup-coloured water surrounded by floating legs of lamb and a huge side of beef, with ten thousand dollars in assorted notes and his briefcase bobbing gently up and down around him.

The iron grip of Viljoen's hand seized his wrist and the handcuff snapped shut. 'Jack Plane, you're under arrest,' said Captain Viljoen in his clipped Afrikaans accent, water still running down his face. He held up the manacled hand triumphantly and the amazed crowd rewarded this bizarre aquatic lunch-time spectacle with a spontaneous roar of applause.

Bill Borden's champagne party was in full swing as the *Princess Pretoria*, latest flagship of the Saf-Marine fleet, ploughed slowly towards Cape Town harbour. The sun had started its slow decline and dipped out of sight behind

Table Mountain, giving the big flat-topped rock a crimson rim.

For Bill it had been a wonderful cruise. Four whole days of fun. He would tell all his banking chums in Johannesburg. As always Bill Borden had been the life and soul of the party. This was his final star turn. French champagne and silver platters of smoked salmon – no expense spared – for all his new-found friends.

It was, like the other parties on the cruise, a formal occasion. The women in colourful silk evening dresses, diamonds flashing from their sun-bronzed bodies, the men immaculate in their white dinner jackets and black bow ties. Waiters twirled silver salvers above their heads as they moved amongst the guests, while others carried bottles of Veuve Cliquot wrapped in white napkins, making sure every glass was full. The noise of the conversation was rising to a crescendo as the party romped into full swing.

No one, least of all, Bill Borden, noticed the black and white police launch cutting through the swirling Cape surf towards the liner. The first time anyone had a clue that something was wrong was when the embarrassed captain of the ship walked stiffly up to Bill Borden in the centre of the party accompanied by Captain Hendrik Viljoen.

'Excuse me, sir,' said the ship's captain apologetically.

'What can I do for you?' said Bill Borden hesitantly, eyeing the police chief.

'William Borden, I am arresting you for attempted fraud in connection with the Amanda mine and the deception and misrepresentation of its future prospects to the minority shareholders of Eastern Mining of which you are chairman.'

Bill Borden's face went white with disbelief and instinctively he gulped the last of the champagne as Captain Viljoen grabbed him by the shoulder and frogmarched him off the deck.

For Bill Borden, the party was over.

Captain Viljoen wound down the window of his unmarked

police car as it pulled quietly to a halt beside another, a short distance from Fred Spillman's house.

'Is he still in there?' he asked the other driver.

The police sergeant nodded. 'He arrived about ten minutes ago. His wife left half an hour earlier.'

Viljoen looked at the clock on his dashboard. 'He must have come home for lunch.'

'Either that or he's tired,' replied the sergeant. 'The maid just pulled the bedroom curtains.'

Viljoen's eyes narrowed. 'Is there a side entrance?'

The officer pointed to a lane running down one side of the garden. 'Over there, Captain.'

Viljoen crossed the road and walked down to a garden gate. He opened it, walked up to the house, and listened. Not a sound. He tried the back door and the kitchen windows, but they were all locked. He moved quietly round to the back of the house, checking windows as he went, and turned the handle of the lounge French doors. The door opened noiselessly and he stepped in. He tiptoed across the lounge into the hall and stood listening. Muffled sounds of movement came from an upstairs bedroom and the captain climbed the wide sweeping stairway to investigate. The noise came from Fred Spillman's bedroom.

Captain Viljoen slowly turned the handle and eased the bedroom door forward until it was half open. Spillman was kneeling on the end of the bed with his back to the door grunting like a rutting bull, while his sturdy, white backside pumped up and down furiously into the spread-eagled body of his black maid Clarissa. He was still wearing a white shirt, pulled halfway up his back, black shoes, and grey trousers concertinaed round his ankles.

Viljoen unclipped his gun from its black leather holster, pulled back the safety catch, and stepped into the room. He gave Spillman's backside a hefty shove with his jackboot, pushing him off the bed onto the floor.

Fred Spillman knelt on the floor, panting at gunpoint, with a short, stubby erection sticking out from under his shirt-tails. He could not move for his feet were trapped in his tangled trouser-legs. The terror and bewilderment in

136

Fred Spillman's eyes were a delight Captain Viljoen savoured for a long time. For Fred Spillman too, the last dance had just ended.

28

New York
5 a.m.

Mark Ashford slept soundly as the grey dawn lightened the master bedroom of his tenth-floor Manhattan penthouse. He lay on the massive circular bed, his legs and arms still entangled around the limbs of two beautiful young girls with long, flowing blonde hair, who slept beside him.

There was money strewn everywhere, all over the bed and across the thick-piled beige carpet, while jewellery, dresses and lingerie hung from the furniture. The room was silent except for the gentle breathing of the girls and Mark Ashford's light snoring.

He had no knowledge that a single, bold-printed, newsflash was being transmitted to the world's financial markets by Reuters ticker tapes which would soon engulf South African Mining in a major controversy that would threaten its existence. 'South African Mining Directors Arrested For Fraud', read the stark message.

The flashpoint was London, where the markets had just opened. The financial community in the City, the big banks who lent to SAM, the dealers and analysts in the stock-market, and the institutional investors who owned most of the shares, saw the newsflash, and held their breath. Then the selling started.

There's nothing quite like the panic that races round the offices of City institutions when a director of a major public company in which they are invested is arrested. But for three directors, one a main-board finance director, one charged with illegal sexual intercourse with his coloured maid, was just too much for the City to swallow in one gulp.

The rush to get out of South African Mining shares turned into a stampede. Grown men, mild-mannered and courteous, supposedly the smartest students of the British private schooling system, fought, pushed, and yelled to sell the stock.

The price didn't fall, it crashed. Wave after wave of selling dropped the price from 147p to 93p in under thirty minutes. The jobbers, the middle men who make a market in the shares, slashed their prices immediately the news broke to 120p, but not even that huge drop deterred sellers, while a host of professional short sellers joined in the jamboree.

It was 4 a.m. when the phone rang in Mark Ashford's apartment, a low, dull buzz that slowly brought him from his slumbers. He extricated his legs and arms from the girls' and reached over the edge of the bed for the phone.

'Yes,' he croaked, his throat dry, his head aching from too much alcohol.

'Mr Ashford?'

'Yes.'

'UPI news desk. Do you have a statement on the arrests?'

For a rare moment Mark Ashford dropped his guard. 'What the hell are you talking about?' he yelled. One of the girls stirred on the bed.

'Fraud, Mr Ashford. Your finance director and two directors have been arrested in South Africa and charged with fraud. Didn't you know?'

'You've just woken me up. It's the middle of the night. I'll call you back in ten minutes.' He replaced the receiver, his mind racing. Something had gone badly wrong. He moved over to the bed and irritably shook the girls.

'OK. Come on, time to go. Wake up, time to go.' One of them sat up sleepily and put her arms round him, while the other crawled round the floor, still half asleep, picking up dollar bills.

'Not now. I'll call you later.'

The girls climbed into their clothes, and stumbled out

of the front door yawning. Mark stepped into the bathroom and wrapped a thick, cotton towel round his waist, then he dialled Fred Spillman's home number in South Africa.

The phone rang in the darkness and Ethel Spillman woke immediately. She had only been asleep a short time for she had spent most of the night waiting to see her husband at the police station. She answered warily.

'Sorry Ethel, I know it's late.'

She recognized Mark Ashford's voice immediately. 'Mark, they've taken him to John Vorster Square. They won't give him bail or the other two . . .' She broke down, crying the words into the phone. 'Fred said I was to tell you Bill gave them the Eastern Mining report.'

'I'll have Fred out of there in no time, I promise you. Trust me, please. I'll call you in a few hours.'

Next he dialled United Press International. 'Night editor,' said a tired, slightly distant voice.

'This is Mark Ashford. I'm holding a press conference at 9 o'clock this morning at the New York office. You might like to send someone.'

'Yes, we'll be there.'

'Will you hold the story till you've heard our side?'

'We wouldn't normally.'

'Look, it could cost you a lot of money.'

Mark Ashford had learnt over the years the one thing that mad newspaper editors reconsider was the threat of libel. Whatever the outcome, it was always expensive and few papers could match the cash of a big company like his.

'All right. We'll wait till after the press conference. But you realize there's nothing to stop any of the other papers using it.'

'My lawyers are talking to them now. If they damage this company by publishing prematurely, they do so at their own risk.'

He phoned Reuters, Associated Press, and then the *Wall Street Journal*. All agreed to hold the story until the press conference. The other newspapers he would worry about later. The news had broken too late for any of them to carry the story that morning and the evening papers would be at the press conference.

He checked the time. It was 4.15 a.m. He had about four hours to put together the press conference. He made a pot of coffee while he thought through a plan of action. He cursed himself for leaving a copy of the report in Johannesburg, particularly with an idiot like Bill Borden. It was a serious error of judgement and he had no one to blame except himself. But was it such an unreasonable mistake? Borden had been a leading bank manager running one of the largest branches in Johannesburg. He knew the company business, had dealt personally with it for years, and had a precise understanding of his non-executive role as chairman of Eastern Mining. The instructions had been clear: put it in your safe and give it to no one.

He took the coffee over to the dining-room table and picked up the phone from the floor. It was time to summon his lieutenants. At a time like this, he needed all the help he could get. Within an hour, they were all there, sitting round the table. By daylight the plan was laid.

At 8.45 a.m. Mark Ashford's black Cadillac pulled out of the basement garage of his apartment block into a barrage of flashing cameras, television lights and reporters. The New York press had turned out in force.

The Cadillac stopped at the kerbside and they clustered round the back window, peering in through the smoked glass of the car door.

'Wait,' Mark Ashford said to his driver and pressed the electric button to lower the window. He leant forward. Lights blazed and a number of microphones were waved in front of him.

'Good morning, gentlemen,' he said smiling.

'What's the fraud, sir?'

'How much has been stolen?'

'Is South African Mining involved?'

Ashford opened the door of the Cadillac and stepped out. 'I'm happy to talk to all of you and answer any questions.' He looked at his solid 18-carat Rolex. 'But as you all know, I have to be at a press conference at the Manhattan hotel, so let me make a brief statement. I was as surprised as anyone to hear the news from Johannesburg. While the nature of the charge sounds serious, I understand it was instigated by two disgruntled shareholders in a subsidiary company, for what I can only describe as technical offences relating to disclosure. I hope that once the South African authorities have received the full facts on the matter, they will think again. And now, if you will excuse me, I'm running late.'

He turned his back on the crowd, stepped back into the Cadillac, and was gone. It was a start. Five minutes and fourteen blocks across Manhattan, his black Cadillac received the same intense press reception as it pulled up at the main entrance to the hotel.

The smile was still in place, but having said hello to the few faces he recognized, Ashford refused to answer any questions.

'If you let me get inside, I can tell you all I know,' he said.

He pushed through the hotel's revolving entrance doors into the foyer, and another barrage of cameras flashed. Behind him the squad of pressmen pushed and swore at each other as they fought to follow him.

'We're fine,' said his publicity director stepping forward to greet him as Mark Ashford approached the entrance to the conference hall. 'They are all in and ready. You have a couple of minutes before you're on.'

'Who's here?' asked Mark quietly.

'Everyone. You know what they're like if they smell scandal.'

'A pack of screaming wolves after blood,' he said grimly. 'I'll just have to tame them. Well, I'm ready if they are.' He strode into the conference hall, and up the carpeted steps to the small podium at one end. He positioned himself before the microphone, and waited for quiet.

Eddie sat right in the middle of the crowd watching him. So this was the man he had come to get even with. It was the first time he had seen Mark Ashford in the flesh. He was a striking-looking man, suavely dressed in a double-breasted pinstripe suit. His black hair and tanned skin gave him a dark, swarthy appearance and he had the presence and authority of a man with a great deal of money and power. It was exactly what Eddie had expected.

'Ladies and gentlemen,' started Mark Ashford. 'I know you've all got deadlines to meet so I'll keep it brief.' There was a ripple of laughter. Television camera lights suddenly lit the podium with a strong, dazzling light.

'You've all seen the wire service stories. Fraud,' he paused, 'is an emotive word. The charges are absurd. No one has taken any money; no company assets are missing or being misused.

'The incident revolves around a complaint to the South African Police by two minority shareholders about an interpretation of a mining report in one of South African Mining's quoted subsidiaries.

'In recent weeks the two complaining shareholders have built up a twenty per cent plus stake in the company concerned, Eastern Mining. They believed a recent drilling programme at the Amanda mine was going to reap rich rewards. A team of drilling rigs on a defunct mine anywhere in South Africa causes local interest, but in a gold mining city like Johannesburg, it can cause a stockmarket furore.'

Eddie listened closely. It was an impressive performance. If he hadn't known better, he might have believed it himself.

'Unfortunately, the presence of the drilling rigs on this particular mine have been misinterpreted. We haven't made a spectacular new discovery – but it was obviously necessary to make sure there was nothing there before we sold off the land.'

Mark Ashford paused, looked round the auditorium and strengthened his delivery.

'We remain confident that once the South African authorities have examined the drilling reports, the fraud charges will be dropped. If there are any new developments we shall be issuing statements immediately.'

He turned across to the publicity man. 'I don't think there's anything I can add, so I'm not going to invite questions. You all know Mort Clark, our press and publicity director, and I'm sure he will be glad to clarify any points you may wish to raise and give you any necessary background information. There are prepared statements for you to collect at the table by the door.'

The television lights went out and Mark Ashford started putting his notes back into the briefcase. Mort Clark stepped forward to meet a handful of journalists coming towards the podium, notebooks at the ready.

It was a good time to leave. From the corner of his eye, Ashford saw that his exit was going to be interrupted by correspondents from the *Financial Times* of London and the *Wall Street Journal*. When he saw there was no escape, he walked straight towards them. 'I'm sorry it was a bit brief,' he said. 'I've got to be at Kennedy in forty-five minutes for a press conference in London this afternoon.'

The *Financial Times* man was the first to speak. 'Well, there are a few points we hoped you would find time to discuss with us,' he said.

Ashford couldn't see a way out. 'Look,' he said, 'I've got to be on that plane. Why don't you ride out to the airport with me. We can talk on the way and I'll have my driver drop you off at your offices afterwards.'

A few more cameras popped as he waved to a small group of photographers waiting by the Cadillac, and then they were inside and away.

Mark slid open a small walnut cocktail cabinet in front of him and took out a silver thermos of hot coffee, three porcelain mugs and a bottle of Black Label. He handed each of the journalists a mug, filled it with coffee and topped it up with a large dollop of whisky. He helped them and himself to sugar and settled back into the black Conolly hide.

'Where would you like to begin?'

The Cadillac floated down the freeway towards Kennedy

airport. The questions came thick and fast, but Mark Ashford had an answer for all of them.

In the Cadillac the telephone purred. Mark Ashford snatched it from its case.

'Yes,' he said curtly.

'I have Peter Newman for you on the other line. Should I switch him through?'

'Yes please.'

Peter Newman was the senior partner of Newman & Newman, South African Mining's London stockbrokers.

Mark turned to the journalists. 'Sorry, it's London and it's urgent. I'll be out of reach for four hours on Concorde.' He was interrupted by Peter Newman's voice.

'Mark?'

'What's happening Peter?'

'Your press conference story came over the wire services here about five minutes ago. The selling seems to have dried up for the moment and the price has firmed 4p to 130p. Some of the bears are closing their short positions.'

'Good.' Mark Ashford glanced at the journalists. It was impossible for them not to listen. 'Pick up any large lines of stock on offer. If you can't find any, go into the market and buy 250,000 shares up to 140p.'

'Right Mark. I'll leave word at your London office.'

Mark Ashford replaced the receiver and turned back to the two journalists in the car. He knew his buying instructions would have been carefully noted.

The lights of the international terminal at Kennedy airport loomed through the damp greyness of the New York morning.

The Cadillac stopped outside the entrance to the terminal. 'Gentlemen, thank you for your time.' He shook both their hands. 'If you need any more information ring me at the London office or speak to my secretary here in New York. She always knows where to get hold of me.'

He slid the bar open again and pointed to the flask of coffee and whisky.

'Help yourselves. The phone is there if you want to ring your offices.'

He turned to the driver, who stood beside him holding a large leather flight bag. 'Take these two gentlemen back to their offices please James.'

'Of course sir,' he said, bowing slightly.

As Mark Ashford disappeared into the crowded airport terminal, a yellow cab drew up behind his Cadillac. Eddie Vandermeer paid his fare, then sauntered through the main entrance of the terminal after him.

29

London
Savoy hotel
12 November
8.30 p.m.

Mark Ashford and Hamish Macfarlane were used to hectic schedules, but they had never experienced anything like today. During each meeting they had been subjected to hours of harrowing questioning about all sorts of corporate matters they would rather not have discussed, first by their main bankers, then the merchant bank and later by the partners of their London stockbroker. They were followed to each place by a permanent entourage of photographers and journalists; and the blazing white lights of television cameras were there each time to greet them.

The pressure of the day showed on Ashford's gaunt face; his skin had turned a pallid grey, and his eyes were bloodshot with dark circles around them.

He yawned, then swallowed a mouthful of whisky.

'Well, where do we go from here, Hamish? We've stopped the bleeding, most of the press seem to be sympathetic and our banks – except the Merchant Bank – believe what they read. Now we've got to get the patient back on his feet.'

'It depends what comes out in South Africa. If the authorities start dragging us through the courts it could turn into a bloody saga. And suppose the South African police go and take a look at the mine?'

'No chance. I've had the Zimbabwean Minister of Mining in my pocket since he took office. Don't forget the war – they'd never let them in.'

'What if they fly over the compound and take photographs?'

'None of that bothers me,' said Mark wearily. 'It's just that bloody report.'

Ashford looked around to see if anyone was within earshot. The candlelit tables were filling up now with theatregoers dressed in their dinner suits and mink wraps for the night out. White-coated food waiters and red-coated wine waiters moved briskly round the dining room and two chefs in starched white aprons and tall, white hats pushed heated trolleys from one table to another.

'Do you think he's press?' asked Mark inclining his head towards Eddie's table in the corner of the restaurant.

Eddie had been watching Mark's table closely, and as soon as he saw him looking round the restaurant, he glanced at the wine list.

Hamish swung round. 'No. He looks too well-heeled to be a reporter.' They turned away.

'If we had the South African foreign minister here,' said Mark tapping his finger firmly on the table, 'we could solve all this right now.'

'We're as close as we can get,' said Hamish peering over Mark's shoulder. 'Here comes Jan.'

Dr Jan Vlaminck looked every bit the spry, clean-cut physician he was, despite the gruelling fourteen-hour flight from Johannesburg.

Mark stood up and shook his hand warmly. 'Good of you to come over, Jan. Sit down here, and let's get you a drink.' He ordered another round of large scotches and once the waiter had left, the doctor turned to Ashford.

'Well, how's it going?'

'So far, so good.'

'What about this report?'

So he knew. Mark Ashford had always admired the doctor's ability to get inside a situation at short notice.

His contacts within South Africa's ruling Nationalist Party were impeccable, and Ashford was glad to see he still knew how to operate them.

'Jan, I'm sure I don't need to tell you there are many ways of interpreting drilling results.'

'It looked pretty conclusive to me.'

The waiter arrived with the first course and the conversation ended uneasily until he left.

'Where do you go from here?' asked Vlaminck.

'Good question. The London merchant bank resigned this morning and the New York one is considering its position. I'm not sure,' continued Mark. 'We've got huge borrowings, and we need the support of the banks. If they withdrew our credit facilities, SAM goes under. These London banks have agreements on their loans, enabling them to call the lot at seven days' notice. Our loans total £680 million. I'd never be able to replace that kind of money in a week.'

'What are the alternatives?' The doctor tried to sound encouraging.

'Beats me,' sighed Mark Ashford. 'There has to be an answer, but I can't see it at the moment.'

He felt depressed. It was the first time he had really admitted it to himself. 'What I have to do is get myself into the game – I have to do a deal with the South African government. I need something the government wants.'

'The atom bomb,' joked Macfarlane.

'They've had it for years,' replied Vlaminck.

'Well, there must be something they haven't got. What about the prime minister? Can we buy him? He can name his price.'

Vlaminck shook his head. 'Every multinational could do that, without all your problems. Why should he risk you?'

'Jan, what does the government want? There must be something?'

'Not money or mineral wealth, South Africa has plenty of both. She doesn't need arms. She manufactures her own, and Israel will sell us anything else.' The doctor paused. 'The only thing South Africa really needs, and in the long term it's going to be a question of survival for her, is acceptance. Acceptance, that is, by the West of her racial policies.'

'Forget it.' Hamish dismissed the idea immediately.

'Let him finish,' said Ashford.

Dr Jan Vlaminck's voice slowed and his Afrikaans' accent thickened as he talked about his mother country. 'South Africa has a problem. We all know it. She has twenty million Africans clamouring for one man, one vote – and as soon as they get it, they'll vote the Afrikaners right out the door. We cannot give blacks the vote – no matter how much we want to. It's as good as giving the country away.' He paused. 'Now, if you can gain a measure of acceptance in England or America, then you have cards to play with. Of that I promise you.'

Mark Ashford leant forward, rested his head in the palms of his hands, and gazed deep in thought across the table. Somewhere in the back of his mind the germ of an idea moved. American acceptance of South Africa he could not accomplish. He didn't have those kind of contacts in America, and it would take too long to organize. The same thing applied to England. But, thought Mark, hitting that rich seam of inventiveness that set him apart from other wealthy men, I do have the black African states around South Africa's borders.

Then he turned to the South African.

'Jan, I don't have the influence or the contacts to deliver the West on a platter. But suppose I could arrange for some of South Africa's black neighbours to start a new initiative of friendship towards South Africa? Suppose one or two heads of state could be persuaded to stand up in their parliaments and make a statement of optimism and friendship towards South Africa?' Mark became enthusiastic. 'A new feeling towards South Africa, a new détente. How does that sound?'

Vlaminck grinned and raised his eyebrows. 'Could you deliver?'

'Maybe,' said Mark thoughtfully. 'We have big companies in sixteen African countries. I know all of the heads of state personally.'

'Could there be trade benefits?'

'I can guarantee it.'

Dr Jan Vlaminck's attitude brightened. 'What you need is a negotiator, someone South Africa will take seriously.'

'Why not me?' said Ashford.

'Suppose they arrest you at the airport?' countered the doctor. 'Can you imagine what your bankers would say then?'

Ashford nodded his head in agreement.

Hamish Macfarlane entered the conversation. 'What about Sir James McCleod? He's an ex-British foreign minister and he's done work for us on a consultancy basis before in African countries.'

'He'd be ideal. He was at Oxford with our foreign minister,' added Vlaminck. 'I think they even shared a room. But would he do it?'

'There's only one way to find out.'

'Do you know where he is, Hamish?'

'In London. I had a drink with him the other night. We were at the same dinner party.'

'Give him a call,' suggested Ashford. 'Ask if we can see him tomorrow – as a matter of urgency. Don't alarm him, or give him any clues. But try to see him first thing.'

Hamish Macfarlane left the dining room to phone, leaving the two other men alone.

'Will you help me, Jan? I need someone like you to lobby those Boers at the top of the Nationalist Party. Even if you can't help me directly, you could keep me in touch with their thinking.'

'Of course, but . . .' He didn't have to say any more. When Mark Ashford did business there was always a 'but'.

'A one-off payment of fifty – any currency – over and above your normal fees and expenses. A special payment regardless of the outcome.'

'Double it and you've got a deal.' Mark was in no position to argue. 'Fifty regardless of outcome. And another fifty if we succeed.'

The doctor leant across the table and squeezed Mark's hand. 'Done.'

'Good. I'll take care of it first thing in the morning.'

'Who's going to negotiate with the African leaders?'

'Hamish. He knows them all. I'm sure the Zambian president will help me. He's an old soldier from way back. Says he wouldn't be president if I hadn't flown him in the guns.'

'And I can help behind the scenes. The government will naturally assume I am working for them, but of course I can report to you daily.'

'Sounds ideal, Jan. We can make the firm offer through Sir James and get their reactions from you. Call me at home in the evenings after eight. You had better use a friend's phone or make sure your scrambler is working.'

Vlaminck nodded. 'I know the form.'

Hamish Macfarlane walked briskly across the dining room and sat down at the table. 'Tonight,' he said gleefully. 'He asked us to use the rear entrance to the house. There's a service road and a gate into the back garden. One of his staff will be waiting for us. He also suggested using a different car just in case the press are on the trail. Doesn't particularly want them hanging around the house.'

Mark Ashford reached across the table for the bottle of '62 Beaune and refilled the glasses.

'Gentlemen,' he said, lifting his glass. 'A chink of light pierces the gloom.'

30

Eddie followed Mark Ashford and Hamish Macfarlane to Sir James McCleod's house, carefully keeping his distance from the Rolls Royce as it swept through the empty London streets, then away from the city and out onto the M4. When the car turned off the road through the tall, wrought-iron gates at the end of a long driveway up to Mark Ashford's country residence, Eddie drove on.

He parked the hired Ford some way away out of sight, under some trees, and made his way back to the house. A high brick wall around the perimeter of the property was not too difficult to climb. It was a cloudy night and Eddie's path through the wood was made difficult by sudden patches of total darkness when the moon slid behind moving banks of cloud. The sudden crack of a dried branch startled him momentarily in the darkness and a bird flapped its way out of the tree-tops in fright. He stopped and listened. Was there someone else in the wood? But he could only hear the distant noise of traffic churning up and down the motorway.

He made his way quickly to a place on the fringe of the wood where he had a clearer view of the massive, grey stone Georgian mansion. It was positioned confidently in the middle of an idyllic parkland setting, surrounded by immaculate lawns and formal gardens. Macfarlane's Rolls was parked at the front door.

He looked around the grounds for signs of security men or dogs, but saw none. He had noticed a light was on at the porter's lodge when he passed the main gates. Eddie hoped Mark Ashford's security didn't extend any further.

He waited beneath the trees for almost an hour watching the house. The wind grew stronger and he guessed the temperature was close to freezing.

He was about to abandon his cover when the porch light suddenly came on, the front door opened and Ashford and Macfarlane walked out to the car. They shook hands and Macfarlane drove away. Then Ashford turned and went back into the house.

Eddie waited till the lights of the car had disappeared, had a last check around for any sign of security men, and then sprinted, half crouched, across the heavily frosted lawn to a tree, about thirty yards from the wood and ducked into its shadow. He glanced around him. Nothing. There was no sound or movement. Only a sudden blustering of wind and the rattle of the branches above him.

A single light lit one corner of the mansion's sombre outline.

Somehow he had to gain entry to the house.

Eddie wanted a confrontation on his terms, with the

element of surprise in his favour, man to man. The apparent lack of security in the grounds hadn't really surprised him, but he felt sure security alarms would be fitted to the doors and windows. He hoped the system would not be turned on upstairs until Mark Ashford went to bed. There were dangers, and he knew it. But he was a gambler – and he might have to wait a long time to find Mark Ashford so relatively unguarded.

The moon came out again from behind the clouds and spotlit the house. Eddie looked for an open window on the ground floor but there was none. His eyes combed the upper storey and stopped finally at a skylight on the main flat roof.

He waited for the cover of the clouds and then made a straight low dash for the porch jutting out at the front of the house.

While he recovered his breath, Eddie tested his weight against the thick, gnarled wisteria. It was old but strong. He looked up at the balcony and pulled himself slowly up towards it. He had climbed roughly his own height before his hand grabbed hold of the slatted stone side of the first floor verandah.

Once there, he stepped back against the side of the house and looked around him. The single light still shone from the end of the house. He stood on the verandah wall, felt for the ridge supporting the guttering and lifted himself up onto the roof. He made his way carefully to the skylight and tried to open it, forcing his fingers under the metal rims of the panes of glass. He worked quickly testing each section of the skylight, but found only one that moved a fraction. He tried it again. There was enough room to get a lever in between the rim and the frame, then he might be able to force it. His eyes darted round the roof floor for a suitable implement, but clouds blocked out the moonlight again and he was left in darkness.

Before he went to bed Mark Ashford permitted himself a small treat he had been saving all day. He poured himself

152

a last brandy, unlocked the wall safe in his study and settled down on the sofa next to the fire with a small pile of share certificates.

The certificates represented his latest stockmarket coup – 19.2 per cent of Eastern Mining, to stack up on top of South African Mining's existing majority stake. But the purchase of the latest holding was particularly satisfying. It had been bought two days earlier from the stock-exchange liquidation committee in charge of winding up the affairs of Vandermeer & Vandermeer. It was Eddie Vandermeer's entire holding in Eastern Mining.

Max Llewellyn had bought it for Mark through a Swiss bank nominee account. The price was eighteen cents, the current market value of the shares in Johannesburg. Mark Ashford chuckled aloud as he sifted through the certificates and saw some of the prices Eddie had paid a few weeks ago.

A light thump from the top of the house distracted him from his gloating pleasure. He walked to the window and pulled back the curtains. The tall conifers around the house had their tops bent to the wind but the garden looked peaceful otherwise. Then he remembered the night a tree was blown over, damaging one side of the house, and thought he'd better investigate.

The best view of the garden was from the bedrooms and, whistling softly to himself, he climbed the lushly carpeted stairway. Halfway up he stopped to turn on the lights. To his utter amazement a figure was hanging by his hands from the skylight over the landing.

He didn't wait to find out who was paying him a surprise visit. He turned on his heels and ran.

Mark Ashford was either going to raise the alarm – or to find a gun. Either way he had to be stopped. Eddie dropped down onto the landing and leapt down the stairs after him. Grabbing a long-necked Chinese porcelain vase from its wall recess he hurled it, base first, at Ashford's head. The vase hit the wall and smashed into pieces. Eddie rounded the sweep of the stairs, caught hold of a second vase, hurled it with full strength, and watched, mildly surprised, as it scored a direct hit on the back of Mark Ashford's head.

Ashford grunted with pain, lurched forward, arms flailing to steady his reeling body. He staggered helplessly down two steps, then his feet missed the bottom stair and he fell forward, knocking over an antique cabinet of crystal glass. He ricocheted sideways, hands still grabbing for a hold, and pulled a slim, rosewood grandfather clock down with him. It crashed to the floor with a booming chime and Mark Ashford's body collapsed unconscious on top of it.

Eddie watched in amazement, still halfway up the stairs. The tinkling of broken glass had stopped, but the deep resonant chime of the grandfather clock still vibrated in the darkness. He looked up and down the hallway for lights. If there was anyone else in the house, they would certainly have appeared by now.

Only the study light shone through the half-opened door at the end of the passageway. He bent down over the unconscious body of Mark Ashford and listened to his deep breathing. He pulled back an eyelid and it closed as soon as he let go. 'You'll have one hell of a headache in the morning, you mother . . .' Eddie said to himself and ran quietly down the corridor.

Mark Ashford's study was just as he had left it. The share certificates were spread across the sofa and the safe door hung open. Eddie picked up the half-filled brandy glass from the table in front of the fire, and drained it in one gulp. He hadn't bargained for such an immediate confrontation with Ashford and still felt a little shocked. But when he leafed through the share certificates, his nervousness disappeared.

'Bastards,' he swore lightly.

Next he went to the wall safe. The bottom was lined several layers thick with packets of money in different currencies. The top front line was fifty-pound notes in packets of £10,000. There were also dollars, marks and Swiss francs.

Above the money was a metal shelf heaped with files,

papers, and large pink cardboard folders bound in legal red ribbon. He took out a single buff-coloured envelope which lay on the top of the pile. His hands shook with excitement. It was Mark Ashford's half of the contract to sell Amanda's newly found gold.

He thought fast. If he took the contract, Ashford would know and take evasive action. If he stole nothing, Ashford would remain suspicious. Play safe, thought Eddie. Make a copy of the contract and take a bundle of money. He wasn't a thief, but he enjoyed helping himself to £50,000 of Mark Ashford's loot. Now he could repay Lucy and have £20,000 pocket money left over. A simple burglary might throw Ashford off the scent. He pocketed five bundles of ten thousand pounds, and took the contract to a photo-copier and shredder standing in a corner of the room. He checked the hallway. Still no one. He went back to the machine, copied each page and turned off the machine. He slipped the contract back in the envelope, and returned it carefully to the same place.

He left the study as he found it, and ran down the hallway. Ashford remained slumped across the grandfather clock. Eddie paused for a second to check he was still breathing, then made for the front door. His hand reached up to open the latch when he noticed a red light glaring at him in the darkness. The alarm system. Ashford had switched it on downstairs, but not upstairs. He studied the panel closely till his eyes grew accustomed to the dark. He found the 'off' switch, turned it and opened the front door. In the moonlight, he saw a guard with an Alsatian walking around the perimeter of the estate. A phone rang some-where near him. Should he answer it? No, let it ring. He pushed the door shut. He waited until the ringing stopped, then opened the door and looked out.

The guard had passed the main gates, moving away from the wood and the place where Eddie parked his car. Eddie watched him till he was out of sight. When he was satisfied it was safe, he ran off across the lawns – the moon his only witness.

Ten minutes later he was on the M4 back to London.

Eddie felt bitterly jubilant. At last he had some indisputable proof of the potential of Amanda. But Mark Ashford's purchase of his Eastern Mining stake was the last straw. He felt guilty that he hadn't taken more interest in the winding up of the family firm. He had been so upset by his father's death, he paid little attention to the mechanics of how it was done. He had found the whole procedure pointless. Now he was seething.

He turned off the motorway at Heathrow airport, returned his car to the hire firm, and bought a ticket for the 9.30 flight to Johannesburg. He had four hours to kill before boarding; he went up to the restaurant, ordered a minute steak and a bottle of '76 Pommard and slept for three hours on a sofa in the passenger lounge.

Shortly before he boarded, he phoned Izzie in Johannesburg and brought him up to date.

'I'm going to see Llewellyn now,' said Izzie. 'The committee of the Johannesburg stock exchange,' he said sarcastically, 'have asked me to give evidence about my dealings in Eastern Mining before your firm went under.'

'What are you going to tell them?' asked Eddie.

'Nothing they don't know already,' laughed Izzie. 'What time does your flight get in?'

'About nine this evening your time.'

'OK, pal. I'll be there.'

31

Izzie Van Royen barged through the tall, polished, pine doors of the committee room of the Johannesburg stock exchange ten minutes late for his nine o'clock appointment. He couldn't have cared less. If he had thought of it before, he would have done it on purpose. The truth was he wanted to get in and out of the inquiry as quickly as possible. Izzie had better things to do than sit and talk all morning to Max Llewellyn and his cronies on the committee. The gold price had just jumped another six dollars the previous night in New York and there was money to be made.

He strode briskly down the long, panel-clad committee room lined with portraits of past presidents.

'Bloody crooks, the lot of them,' said Izzie to himself as he glanced momentarily down the line of gilt frames each with a small brass lamp above it.

But the biggest crook of all, and the one he disliked the most, sat like a well-fed buddha on the ornately carved president's chair at the centre of the committee-room table. Max Llewellyn was feeling quietly confident. If the trading floor was Izzie's domain, this was his.

'Now you've arrived, Mr Van Royen,' he said, pulling up a starched white shirt cuff, and studying his quartz digital, 'we can start.'

Izzie ignored the sarcasm and marched straight to a chair placed a short distance in front of the committee. He sat down and stared disdainfully at the men in front of him.

'Is there an ashtray?' he asked.

'Over there,' replied Max pointing to several on top of a cornerbar at one side of the room.

Izzie made no move.

He wants me to get it, thought Max astonished. He turned to the clerk. 'I wonder if you would pass Mr Van Royen an ashtray.'

Max was not to be thrown.

'Perhaps I should start by outlining the rules governing this inquiry,' he started.

'I am well aware of the rules.'

Izzie drew heavily on his cigarette and exhaled a long plume of grey smoke straight at Max.

'Right then. The first question my committee wishes to put to you, Mr Van Royen, is why you dealt so actively in Eastern Mining prior to the sudden price surge – and then again just before the price collapse?'

Max's podgy fingers plucked a piece of paper from the file in front of him and he held it up. 'We have a complete list of your firm's dealings.'

Izzie took a long final draw from his cigarette, and ignoring the ashtray, stamped out the butt on the gleaming wooden floor. He smiled at Max sardonically.

'Mr President. I am a complex man and I buy shares for many different reasons,' he said. 'I don't think I should take up this committee's time with irrelevant detail. However, if you insist. . . . Sometimes I buy shares because dishonest directors of public companies ring me up and ask me to buy ahead of results or a takeover. Sometimes I buy them because I hear stories in the market about certain member firms buying heavily then pushing the price up. Sometimes I buy shares because mining houses try to steal them from minorities. And sometimes I buy because I plain like the look of a stock. . . . There are many reasons why I buy shares, Mr President.'

Max Llewellyn bristled with anger. 'Mr Van Royen, we are here on an extremely serious investigation. My committee and I wish to know specifically why you bought shares in Eastern Mining before the sudden bout of speculation that sent the share price through the roof.' He shouted the last three words, and his neck and cheeks reddened in anger.

Izzie was starting to enjoy himself. He lifted himself out of the chair and paced up and down the length of the table.

'Take the other morning for instance,' he continued, ignoring Llewellyn's question. 'I was sitting on the can reading about the directors of SAM being arrested, and decided it was time to start selling SAM shares. Doesn't your firm act for SAM, Mr President?'

Max Llewellyn's voice sharpened. 'That is not what we are here to discuss. We want to know why you bought Eastern Mining shares at the precise moment you did?'

Izzie swung round and faced his interrogator.

'How dare you?' he shouted.

Max was caught off his guard. Izzie moved in closer to him.

'You call me in here to question me in front of your friends?' Izzie's fiery eyes flashed to the men sitting either side of Max. 'You know better than anyone else why Vandermeer's went under. You and Mark Ashford schemed it, dumped the share price, and bought Vandermeer's stake for nothing.'

Llewellyn rose to his feet. 'I will not have my firm's reputation talked about like this.'

Izzie smiled, but didn't budge an inch.

'Don't try it on, Max. I've seen the share transfers. One more word from you and you're inside with your friends from SAM.'

He grabbed Max by his president's tie, and pulled him across the table. He held Max's reddening face six inches away and stared straight into his frightened baby-blue eyes. 'I've got two words to say to you Mr President,' Izzie sneered.

'Get fucked.'

32

Cape Town
Mount Nelson hotel
12.15 p.m.

Sir James McCleod, former British foreign minister under the last Labour government, and newly appointed special envoy for Mark Ashford, stood on the sun-soaked balcony of his suite at the Mount Nelson waiting for the second most powerful man in the South African government to arrive. It was an important meeting for Sir James as it would probably determine the fate of the third largest mining group in the world, but more importantly for Sir James it promised to make him a rich man.

Mark Ashford had called from New York a few minutes earlier to wish him good luck and confirm the payment fees to his bank in Lichtenstein. As he gazed down the side of Table Mountain at Cape Town's sparkling city centre with its white office blocks, port, and on round to the long stretches of beach, he mused on the successful deal he had struck for himself. True, he had the advantage, but anyone who could turn an advantage over Mark Ashford into hard cash should consider themselves fortunate.

Sir James had listened to Mark's ideas when they met, but came straight to the point. 'How much Mark? That basically is what it boils down to.'

The answer was a straight two hundred thousand pounds no matter what the outcome. On release from South Africa and arrival in New York, Sir James would immediately become the owner of 5 per cent of the issued share capital of South African Mining. It would make him a multi-millionaire. That was one of Mark's very special payments.

But beneath the calm, diplomatic exterior, Sir James felt slightly uneasy. It was the first time he had negotiated for such high personal stakes and this was without the backing and authority of the British government.

A white Mercedes flying the orange, white and blue flag of South Africa on its bonnet swept up the steep, tree-lined drive to the hotel. There was no police escort as Willem Van den Bergh was not on official business. The car stopped outside the white marble steps leading up to the hotel entrance and Sir James skipped lightly down the single flight of stairs to meet his former room-mate at Oxford.

Willem Van den Bergh could not walk into a room and avoid being noticed. It wasn't just that he was tall, with wide shoulders supporting a huge granite-like head, but he had the bearing of a man who wielded enormous power. His fellow politicians nicknamed him 'The Bear'.

A much revered Afrikaner, he moved freely around the innermost power base of the ruling Nationalist party shaping international and domestic policy for South Africa.

Sir James met him as he pushed through the swing doors into the foyer.

'*Meneer*,' said Willem Van den Bergh, the depth of his resonant voice gave the word extra warmth. He shook Sir James's thin manicured hand with a strong squeeze. 'James,' he beamed, 'you have been away from here much too long.'

'It's wonderful to see you, Willem, I miss this place too.'

They walked down the foyer with its big, white marble pillars, low hanging colonial fans swishing noiselessly and the mass of green plants and climbing vines, into the enormous lounge and bar. Sir James pointed to some glass doors leading out into the gardens. They talked briefly of the old days at Oxford, made polite inquiries about each other's families until they came to a table beneath a Jacaranda tree near the pool. A liveried waiter served them chilled Lanson Black Label from a silver ice bucket and stand.

Willem raised his glass. 'To the good old days.'

He laughed a great belly laugh.

'To our friendship,' followed Sir James quickly.

Willem Van den Bergh put his glass down. 'If you won't live here, Jimmy, you should come and see us more often.' His arms swept round the gardens and pool. 'This place is paradise, particularly during your dreary British winter. South Africa needs friends with your influence in Washington and Europe. We would make you most welcome.'

His voice tailed off and he glanced round him, but the waiter had retired discreetly.

'You know,' he said confidentially, 'the prime minister and I have never forgotten the time you spoke to Kissinger about . . .'

Sir James raised his hand and laughed. 'Willem,' he said. 'We all agreed we would never mention it again.' He paused. 'The point is – can you help us now?'

'I don't know. . . . It's a difficult one.' The warmth had gone from Willem's voice. 'If it was up to my department, perhaps I would find a way. The trouble is the case is already in the courts. All three men have been remanded without bail and the trial hearing dates are due to be set.'

Sir James watched his former room-mate closely. The South African was a master at hiding his real intentions. Not a trace showed on his enigmatic face.

Willem Van den Bergh leant his huge bear's shoulders across the table and inclined his great granite head closer to Sir James.

'The trouble is Jimmy, you can do most things in this country, but you can't mess around with the judicial system. It is supposed to be beyond reproach. The PM believes that strongly.'

'Of course,' said Sir James. 'I appreciate your position.'

'Normally Mark would do it with no strings attached – he's been talking to your neighbours for months about it. But the arrests have put the whole company under a cloud. Mark and his directors are confident no fraud has been committed and the courts will come to the same conclusion. But you and I know perfectly well that if the case takes the usual time to go through the courts there won't be a South African Mining left at the end of it.'

'How would you start?'

'I have personally met the heads of state of Botswana and Zambia in London. They promised me their support. The Zambian prime minister will make a major policy speech to his parliament. He is president of the OAU this year. . . . It will carry a lot of weight.'

Van den Bergh nodded his agreement. It would be reported worldwide.

'But the problem is still how to remove the case from the judicial system,' he said.

'You don't have to. Let them go home on bail, set up an inquiry, and then drop all charges.'

Van den Bergh considered the position for about thirty seconds.

'We'll see,' he said. 'I'll talk to the PM. He must decide.'

Sir James felt like a batsman with his first half century under his belt as he stood up and drained his glass.

'Come on Willem. I've got the best lobsters in the Cape being prepared for us. We can talk more over lunch.'

At long last, thought Sir James as he walked through the gardens to the restaurant, I'm going to be a rich man.

While Sir James McCleod and Willem Van den Bergh cracked lobster claws in the Grill Room of the Mount

Royal, another important meeting was taking place two miles away across the city in the offices of the Chief Minister of Justice.

Eddie arrived back from London keen to pass the copy of Mark Ashford's contract over to the authorities. He preferred not to hand it over cold to the police, bearing in mind how he acquired it. Instead he contacted a friend and former client who worked in the Minister of Justice's office in Cape Town. Then he and Izzie flew to the Cape to see him.

John Walsh was second generation English. Mild mannered and gently spoken, he was balding and wore thick rounded glasses. Eddie had known him since his schooldays in the Cape and he was one of Eddie's few clients who had been genuinely sympathetic when Vander-meer's went under.

Eddie and Izzie sat in John Walsh's office watching him leaf through a light blue folder.

The office reminded Eddie of Walsh's study at school. One wall was completely shelved holding rows of law books, the other was scattered with lines of black-framed professional certificates hanging unceremoniously from pieces of string. The room was neat, spartan and decorated in fading shades of ochre.

John Walsh turned the last page of his department's report, closed the folder and looked across his desk at Eddie.

'I don't know what you're worried about. The evidence seems overwhelming,' he said. 'I'm glad I'm not being instructed.'

'Well, it's just that the whole thing's suddenly gone quiet.'

'Quiet as church mice,' Izzie grinned.

'There's always a lull between arrest and a case being heard,' said the assistant minister. 'There's a lot of boring paperwork to go through.'

Eddie opened the briefcase at his feet and took out the copy of the contract he had taken from Mark Ashford's safe.

'Then there's this,' he said.

Walsh read it quickly. 'Where on earth did you get it?' he asked.

Eddie told him the truth.

'So he pre-sold the gold at Amanda on a long-term contract?'

Eddie nodded.

'What do you think it says?' added Izzie sourly. Izzie was never at his best with officialdom, and he never trusted strangers.

John Walsh shot him a glance, then turned back to the contract.

'And you're absolutely sure this is authentic?'

'Absolutely,' said Eddie.

'I'll make a copy and return it.'

At the door John Walsh told Eddie, 'I don't know what you're worried about. This contract will make it almost impossible to defend.'

He held Eddie's arm firmly. 'It's an open and shut case. A baboon could try it.'

33

It was late afternoon before Willem Van den Bergh left the Mount Nelson and drove through the rich green valleys and vineyards outside Cape Town to Stellenbosch, the Cape Dutch university town nestling beneath the great Stellenbosch mountains. The vineyards and farms run for miles through the valley floors and the rows of vines stretch up onto the lower slopes.

He had driven the route many times before but this evening the mid-summer splendour of the countryside and the potential of his mission gave him a rare sense of excitement. It was just before six as he turned into the long straight driveway up to the classic Dutch farmhouse that was the prime minister's private residence.

He slowed down at the security gate, waved to the guard,

and drove on up to the house. The stout, slightly stooping figure of the prime minister was waiting to greet him.

Johannes Petrus Stein had been cutting his roses. He stood at the balcony steps, a flower basket of pink and yellow cut blooms in one hand, a pair of rose cutters in the other. He wore a floppy straw hat pulled deep down on his forehead, white shirt and cream flannel trousers held up by an ageing necktie knotted tightly to one side of his waist.

'*Meneer*,' he welcomed Van den Bergh, and led him to some easy chairs at one end of the balcony. He rang the small table bell and a black servant appeared instantly, wearing a white coat, white gloves, and carrying a small silver tray.

'What will you take, man?' asked the prime minister in Afrikaans.

'White wine, please,' Willem told the waiter.

'Two,' said the prime minister. 'Bring us a bottle of Grunberger. The '78.'

Johannes Stein leant back in his chair and his voice dropped to a tone of confidentiality. 'Well, what did the Englander have to say for himself?'

'He doesn't like us locking up his directors,' Van den Bergh laughed.

'It's about time some of those Englanders were caught,' replied the PM. 'They've been getting away with it for years. The mining houses are the biggest crooks of the lot.'

'Our people are no different,' Willem reasoned. 'If anything they are worse – they need the money more. We know it goes on, we've known it for years.'

The waiter returned, poured two glasses and left.

'Good luck, Willem,' said the prime minister.

'*Suid Afrika*,' toasted Willem Van den Bergh. 'Ashford has proposed a deal,' he said. 'Normally, I would have said no. But this one could affect our father-land.'

Johannes Stein sat listening quietly, his eyes alert, his fleshy drink-reddened face impassive.

'Good for us, but good for him too, no doubt.'

Willem looked at him with a twinkle in his eye. 'It's an

intriguing deal. And a brilliant one.' He sat back in his chair holding the half-filled glass of wine in his hand. 'Let the directors go, drop all charges and South African Mining will guarantee a new era of acceptance, a new détente with our troublesome neighbours.'

'Can they deliver?'

'Sir James McCleod, once a British foreign minister is negotiating on their behalf. He gave me his word they can.'

The PM was impressed. He had a great deal of respect for Sir James.

Willem outlined the discussions at the Mount Nelson until the PM interrupted.

'There's one major problem – the case is already in the courts. That means interfering with the legal system. You know how I feel about that.'

'Of course. But I think we should consider the position very carefully. If our neighbours stand together before the rest of the world and say give South Africa a chance, it makes it a damned sight harder for the Western world to criticize us. Trade and political embargoes might conceivably be lifted. . . . I can make the necessary arrangements with the attorney general to "withdraw" the charges. Legally, that means we can always resurrect them.'

'You seem to have worked it all out.' Stein refilled their glasses.

'The opportunity seems too good to miss. South African Mining has enormous interests in this country. If they don't deliver, well . . .'

The prime minister nodded. 'I'm not entirely convinced, but do it. I don't want to know the details. If I am ever asked in parliament I want no knowledge of it.' He pointed a stubby finger at his foreign minister. 'If it ever comes out, I'll have your head.'

Willem stood up. 'Of course,' he said.

'Won't you finish the bottle with me?' asked the Prime Minister.

'Thank you, Johannes,' he said, shaking his hand. 'But there is much to do.'

34

The president of the one-party state of Zambia sat in the carved wooden throne on a raised dais before his parliament, waiting for the discordant blaring of trumpets that announced his arrival to subside.

Today was a special day, the twentieth anniversary of Zambian independence and the importance of the event was not lost on the representatives of his five million people, sitting in a wide circle of seats before him. The forty or so loyal subjects, resplendent in their brightly coloured robes, waited expectantly for their president to speak. He was the grand old man of Zambian politics, and had sustained his benevolent dictatorship ever since he led his people to independence.

The trumpeters, a small detachment from the president's own royal guard, let rip a final blast from the gallery above the throne, then sat down quietly.

All eyes fell on the president, his flowing gown of cream silk gathered around him, arms resting easily along the red velvet arm-rests of his throne. A heavy gold-chained onyx watch, the first present Mark Ashford ever gave him, hung loosely from his wrist. In his other hand he twirled absent-mindedly a short rosewood staff, tipped with long leather thongs, a tribal symbol of power.

The president had met Ashford many years earlier while still a guerilla commander fighting in the bush in southern Zambia where South African Mining owned and operated copper mines. The president's forces controlled Zambia's rich copper region, including the railway out of the country for export. So long as his guerilla forces were in control, the long line of trucks crammed with sheets of refined copper remained in the siding beside the huge, iron-clad smelter at the head of South African Mining's Zambian copper mines.

Mark Ashford negotiated. A free passage for his copper in return for arms bought with a percentage of the profits from each train load. Both men kept their word. The trains got through and the guerilla commander received his guns. Mutual respect led to friendship and during the two years before he came to power, all of the president's weaponry was supplied indirectly by South African Mining, bought with advance payments from copper sales.

The president never forgot a friend. As he rose, he wrapped his silk robe across his shoulder and walked towards the microphone to deliver his Independence Day address. Excitement ignited into an outburst of applause and the audience stood up clapping and cheering. He waited for a minute, then raised his staff and they fell silent.

'It is twenty years ago today, our people gained independence from the British. Many things have changed for the better. We have food, our children receive proper education. We are free to live our lives in our own country and make our own laws. Many things have changed and we are a happier nation for them.' The president frowned.

'But some things have not changed. Ten years ago we lived our lives in the shadow and fear of our powerful white neighbour, South Africa. That was the case when I came to power and that is still the case now. And it goes back even further. For nearly a century, this land of ours, Africa, has been embroiled in a battle of supremacy between blacks and whites. Many battles have been fought, many lives have been lost on both sides. The blood would fill our rivers in the drought, the suffering would make mountains of misery.'

He stopped and looked round the parliament. 'South Africa is rich and powerful and we black African states on her border fear her as an aggressor.' His voice grew firmer. 'In the past I have been in the forefront of black African leaders to attack South Africa. We are fearful of her and we despise her policies of apartheid against her black and coloured people.

'But now,' he reasoned, 'I am an old man of sixty-eight and I ask myself how long must I fear and condemn this neighbour of ours? How many years is the struggle between black and white to continue?' He paused to let his message sink home.

'With age comes wisdom. When I look back over the ten years of our history I am saddened by our relationship with South Africa. We should be good neighbours. We could work together. We should encourage any move to dismantle apartheid and not simply pour scorn on it.' He shook his head slowly. 'There has to be another way, we have to find a common path. The black African states cannot live for ever in Southern Africa fearful of its neighbour's military might. It is time to make a fresh start. It is time for dialogue between the black African states and South Africa. It is time we offered a hand of friendship and solved our differences in a spirit of conciliation.'

'Today, on the anniversary of our independence my message to you, to the leaders of the other black African states and to South Africa itself, is this: We must find a way to live together in peace. We must find a way of solving our differences and of helping each other. We must look at the old problems with new eyes and we must forge a new spirit of détente between our nations.'

Cape Town
21 December
2.30 p.m.

As he rose to make the echo speech in parliament three days before it recessed for the Christmas break, prime minister Johannes Petrus Stein was well aware he would be making history. Political gossip had been rife in Cape Town since the anniversary speech of the president of Zambia a few days earlier, and there had been speculation in the newspapers of a new spirit of détente between South

Africa and the black African states surrounding its borders.

A rumour that a Zambian envoy had been sent to Pretoria for secret talks with the prime minister came as no surprise, while other black African leaders welcomed the new détente with South Africa.

Parliament in Cape Town was packed to capacity for the PM's speech and the demand for access to the parliamentary press gallery was so great that an emergency press room was set up next door and the speech relayed to it.

The prime minister forsook his native Afrikaans and spoke ponderously in English, for the benefit of foreign correspondents.

'Mr Speaker, ladies and gentlemen of the House, as you know, today is our last sitting before the Christmas recess and I feel a duty to talk to you of important events taking place for this our fatherland, South Africa.

'If you were to ask me my views of the future of Southern Africa, I would say I have a great deal of confidence and optimism. It is a developing continent, rich in unexploited ore and raw materials.

'But if you were to ask me what Southern Africa's greatest need is today, I would have to say peace and stability. We are at a crossroads with our black neighbours and with our own black population. For a long time now we have been treated as the international whipping boy in world politics for our policies of apartheid. As with everything else in South Africa these policies are changing, but few political leaders in places like the United Nations will give us any credit for this.'

The prime minister paused to take off his gold half-rimmed glasses before making his crucial point.

'I was therefore gladdened to hear the speech made by the Zambian president a few days ago. I took careful note of what he said and thank him publicly. He is the voice of reason for which we have long been waiting.

'He is a much regarded leader among the front-line states, and I offer him the hand of friendship and an invitation to this country. Let us talk, let us settle our differences and let us all live in peace.'

35

Eddie breaststroked lazily through the cool water watching it ripple out to the edge of the garden pool. It was six o'clock in the morning, the last Sunday before Christmas.

Lucy and the two girls were asleep in the house. The garden was quiet and a thin mist still hung over the lawns. The days were moving into midsummer and the sky was bright blue, though the sun was not yet visible.

More and more these early mornings, Eddie thought about his father. He cursed himself for the way he died, and the disgrace of the firm being 'hammered'. It hurt deeply, but each time he came to the same conclusion – there was nothing he could do. He was lucky to keep his house and car. Fortunately, he had had the foresight to put the house in Lucy's name. Every penny from the business went to pay the bank for his Eastern Mining stake.

Eddie had enough cash for his short-term needs, but he didn't have a job, and there was no immediate prospects of getting one. The place of work he loved, the stockmarket, was technically out of bounds. A partner 'hammered' from the exchange, could never go back. It would even be difficult becoming a member of the New York or London exchange.

He liked the idea of America but his best connections from his Cazenove days were in London. He set himself a deadline. He would decide by the end of Christmas.

From across the dew-laden lawn he heard the ring of the patio phone. Who would call at this time? He lifted himself quickly out of the pool, pulled on his towelling robe, and ran across the wet grass to answer it.

'They've dropped all charges and flown the bastards home.' The voice was unmistakably Izzie's.

'Are you kidding? They can't . . .' exclaimed Eddie.

'Viljoen rang me. They flew all three to New York last night. There was nothing he could do. His commanding

171

officer was called into the attorney general's office late on Friday and told to make arrangements.'

'But what about the stuff I gave Walsh?'

'How do I know? You speak to him.'

'I'll call you later.'

Eddie went into the house, looked up Walsh's number and dialled it.

'Yes?' said John Walsh drowsily.

'It's Eddie Vandermeer.'

'Who?'

'Eddie. Wake up John. The fraud charges. School.'

'Oh, Eddie. Yes. . . . I heard last night.' His voice sounded more alert. 'It's difficult talking now. Can you come down?'

Eddie guessed he didn't want to discuss it on the phone. Did the police even bug assistant ministers' phones?

'I can, but there are no flights today – it's Sunday.'

'Drive. It's after six now. If you left in half an hour you could be here this evening and drive back tomorrow.'

Eddie thought quickly. Johannesburg to Cape Town was a good fourteen hours even in his car. He thought of the Porsche sitting in the garage. A long drive but . . . an enjoyable one. He hadn't given the car a good workout for weeks.

'I'll see you in the bar of the Mount Nelson at nine for dinner. Can you book me a room for the night when the desk opens?'

'Sure. I have to go to the airport this evening. I'll make it as close as I can.'

Eddie went upstairs, showered, packed an overnight bag and said goodbye to a warm, drowsy Lucy.

'Ring me this evening darling when you arrive,' she said sleepily, 'or I'll worry about you.'

He took her warm, soft body in his arms, kissed her and tiptoed out of the bedroom.

The Porsche leapt into life when he switched on the ignition and moments later he turned out of his driveway and drove through the deserted streets of Houghton to the freeway, out of the city, and due south to the Cape.

172

It was six forty. Once clear of the city he slipped on a tape and settled back to put the car through its paces.

John Walsh leant across the dinner table, his round owlish glasses halfway down his nose. 'When I told you a baboon could try it,' he said emphatically, 'I didn't know a baboon would try it.'

'So what goes on? The police have a cast-iron case and let them go. I don't understand it.' Eddie shrugged.

'Me neither. I phoned the attorney general at home as soon as I heard. He was so touchy, anyone would think I wanted to know when he last slept with his wife.'

'Where's the contract?' demanded Eddie.

'America.'

'What? I told you never to . . .'

'Eddie, wait a minute. Hear me out. I told you I was going to the airport?'

'Right.'

'My sister. She's married to a lawyer and has gone back to New York. He's South African by birth. I went through college with him. But the big news for you is he works for the Government Securities and Exchange Commission.'

'Did you tell him the whole story?'

John Walsh nodded confirmation. 'Spoke to him on the phone at the airport.'

Eddie was impressed. If the action was stymied in South Africa, what better tactic than to open up on a new front. Mark Ashford would have little chance of doing a deal with the officers of the SEC.

'Will he do anything?'

'Maybe. He can check the authenticity of the contract with . . .'

'You didn't mention Pierre Bouchard's name.'

'Of course not. On something like this they would deal with the chairman.'

'So now we sit and wait?'

John Walsh shook his head. 'You wait. There's nothing more I can do – I don't want to be involved any further.

If they pursue Ashford, all well and good. If they don't . . .'
John Walsh sounded indifferent, 'it's tough luck on you.'

And that seemed to close the conversation about Mark
Ashford. They had dinner, laughed about some of the
school exploits of friends they had kept in touch with, and
shortly before 11 p.m. Eddie went up to bed. He made a
call to Lucy, then Pierre Bouchard in New York before
turning out the light. He fell asleep almost immediately.

Next morning, he woke as usual at daybreak. He thought
about going for a swim, but decided not to. It was Monday,
the stockmarkets would be open and he had a long drive
back to Johannesburg. He drank a pot of coffee in his room
while he packed and dressed, paid his bill and left the hotel
without breakfast.

His back and shoulders were still a bit stiff from the
drive down but the thoroughbred feel of the car made up
for the discomfort. He was clear of Cape Town in minutes,
heading across the Cape plain to the Garden Route and
the Paarl valley wine country. Then up into the moun
tains and down across the hot red Karoo Dessert to
Johannesburg.

There was no traffic on the road so Eddie let the Porsche
rip. He slipped from fourth to third and accelerated hard.
The car roared up to 100 m.p.h. in seconds, then onwards
in a surge to 140 m.p.h. The wide Pirelli 6s clamped the
road and Eddie felt the body of the car flatten as it sped
down the motorway.

He turned onto the Garden Route, and saw a figure
standing on the side of the motorway, about a mile away.
As he came closer he saw it was an African waiting by the
roadside. He wore a red shirt tied in a knot round his
waist, blue shorts and no shoes. He carried a white plastic
bag. As soon as he saw the car, he waved his arms and
jumped up and down. At the last moment he stuck his
thumb out for a lift.

Eddie slid the gear lever from fifth to third, pushed hard
on the brakes and with the engine whining, screeched to a
halt in a cloud of swirling dust.

He leant across the passenger seat and opened the door.

'Where are you going?' he asked.

The African was still jumping up and down, his face beaming. He stopped, bent down and spoke to Eddie. 'You mean, boss, I can come in the car?'

'Where do you think I mean? On the roof rack?'

The African's face lit up in a huge smile. 'Yeah, yeah,' he said excitedly opening the door and clambering in.

'But where to?' Eddie asked again.

'Straight,' pointed the African. 'About ten miles.'

'You'd better put this on,' said Eddie winding a seat belt round him.

The car roared away in first, and Eddie changed gear at maximum revs.

'Aiyee,' laughed the African, in disbelief at the speed, and slapped his knees.

'What's your name?' said Eddie.

'Billy,' he said slowly, slightly slurring the word. 'My name is Billy.' Eddie turned sideways and Billy gave him a big smile. His eyes were badly bloodshot.

'Where did you get those red eyes, Billy?'

'Dagga, boss,' he said lifting the white plastic bag he held between his feet and opening it. Momentarily Eddie took his eyes off the road and peered into the bag.

'Jesus, where did you get all that from?' Dagga is the African name for marijuana. Eddie hadn't smoked it since his college days in the Cape. Nor had he ever seen so much.

'You want some, boss?'

'No thanks,' he said firmly. 'It's a long way to Johannesburg.'

Eddie put on a tape and Billy swayed and sang to the music, anchored by his seat belt. He knew the words to whatever song came on. Every time Eddie accelerated, he shrieked with excitement.

Billy was a bright, warm character who smiled easily revealing a large gap in the middle of his yellow-stained front teeth.

They drove for half an hour then he pointed to a group of round, strawroofed huts on the side of a hill.

'This is my home. I will leave you now.'

Eddie pulled over to the side of the road, unclipped Billy's seat belt and watched him get out of the car.

'*Hamba Kahle*,' he told Billy. 'It means "go in peace".'

'Thank you my boss,' he beamed. He put his hand in his jacket pocket, pulled out a handful of rolled cigarettes and threw them on the passenger seat.

'It's a long way to Johannesburg,' he chuckled and slammed the car door. Eddie waved goodbye, revved the engine, and was gone, leaving Billy waving and dancing on the roadside. Half a mile down the road Eddie looked in his mirror. Billy was still waving. He glanced down at the hand-rolled cigarettes on the passenger seat. Should he?

The sun was up and he felt the first warmth of the day through the glass of the windscreen. The road was long and straight and was starting to climb out of the flat coastal plain around Cape Town, up into the foothills of the Cape Mountains. The countryside rose and fell in long wide sweeps as far as Eddie could see. The fields were a patch-work of yellow cornfields and green maize, while red, yellow and white wild flowers covered the hillsides. In the middle distance loomed the towering outline of the Cape Mountains, clear-cut and blue.

The Garden Route was still very empty and Eddie only passed a car every two or three miles.

He reached down, picked up one of the rolled cigarettes and lit it. The smoke was mild and sweet and smelt of hay. He inhaled three or four times and then flicked the half burnt cigarette out of the window. Durban Poison, Eddie remembered, had a reputation for blowing your head off.

He felt nothing for the first few minutes then he started to feel relaxed, detached and slightly euphoric. The music became clearer and more resonant. He sighed deeply and felt the tension go out of his body.

But despite the pleasant, floating sensation his thoughts turned back to Mark Ashford and SAM. He could not believe the South African authorities would just let them go. Ashford must have done a deal. Although surely he didn't have that kind of power with governments? The government ran him like they did any other multinational.

Could it have been a bribe? But what would a powerful politician in a government that produced some 80 per cent of the world's gold need? What could he possibly have offered?

Whatever fix Mark Ashford had arranged, Eddie felt sure he could not repeat it in America. Suppose the SEC didn't do anything? How could he make them? Did he need to? Then he remembered one of Izzie's favourite tricks and he clicked his fingers loudly.

'I should go short,' he said to himself. 'Going short' is a difficult concept for some investors, but to most professionals like Eddie it is a reflex reaction to bad news. You sell shares you don't own and buy them back when the price falls. It is the reverse of buying shares in the hope they will go up. Expected bad news normally brings out the short-sellers.

The gambler in Eddie started to buzz. And as always, the arguments made sense. News of an SEC investigation for fraud would almost certainly hit SAM's share price. And there were ways of 'leaking' the news.

He was climbing steeply now into the mountains. His throat felt dry and he suddenly felt ravenously hungry. He pulled over to a restaurant perched on a bend in the road overlooking a stunning view of green valleys and tumbling waterfalls.

He was the only person there. He picked a table by the window, ordered breakfast from the solitary black waiter, and went over to the public phone in the corner. He dialled Izzie's office number.

'What have you got?' asked Izzie.

'He passed the contract to the SEC.'

'Wonderful,' exclaimed Izzie sarcastically. 'Why did they let them go?'

'He doesn't know. It was a top-level decision by the attorney general.'

'Izzie, I'm going short. Sell me 50,000 South African Mining.'

'They'll go higher on the release when the market opens.'

'Sure. Wait thirty minutes, then do them.'

The line went dead. Eddie wasn't sure whether it was because of his suggestion on how to deal, or Izzie's prompt professionalism.

He had breakfast, paid his bill, and got back on the road. The Garden Route climbed steadily higher and then Eddie was up in the mountains. He drove thirty miles through the yellow wood forests until he saw a phone box. He stopped, leaving the engine running. The coins went in, two rings and Izzie's raucous voice was there shouting against the din of the market.

'I've done you 25,000 at six rand. It opened at four rand and is trading at,' he paused to check the prices board, 'seven rand.'

'Fine. Another twenty-five at seven. I'll call you in an hour.'

This time Eddie hung up. It was a measure of their friendship, he thought, that Izzie hadn't asked how he was going to pay for them if the transaction went wrong.

He drove through the mountains for another hour, through the lush, wet vegetation of the rain forests with the tall yellow-woods stretching ever higher for a share of the light, then called Izzie again.

'I've done another 25,000 at seven rand. The stock is trading at eight rand.'

'Average me out with 50,000 at eight rand. It can't keep going up like this.'

'For Christ's sake man,' yelled Izzie. This time he was rattled. 'You're short of R350,000 worth of gold shares in the biggest gold boom in history and now you want to make it R700,000.'

'There's no way the stock can keep going up. If it goes wrong I'll sell my house.'

'Look Eddie, if you go out a second time, that's it. Once people forgive. Twice, in two months – never.'

'Since when were you against going short?'

'I'm not. But you've already kissed your own business goodbye and now you're in danger of blowing mine.'

'The house is worth half a million. If SAM go over twelve rand, I'll sell it.'

'You're a fucking madman,' said Izzie, and hung up.

He drove for another two hours, then stopped for a beer at a roadside bar. It was mid-morning now, and the sun was directly overhead, beating down with its full mid-summer strength. Eddie unclipped the roof of the car, and pulled off his shirt.

By lunchtime, the Porsche was zigzagging its way down the long, twisting route from the mountains into the Karoo, the hot flat red desert between the Cape Mountains and the mountain kingdom of Lesotho, six hours from Johannesburg. Not even the wind-rush from the car cooled the burning on his shoulders.

At the first small Karoo town, he stopped for petrol, a couple more cold beers and a steak. Then he sauntered across the road to the hotel.

'Can I make a call to New York?' he asked. The white receptionist pointed to a phone cubicle next to the entrance to the bar.

'It's Eddie, I'm calling from South Africa.'

'*Mon ami* – how are you?'

'Fine thanks. Pierre, I want you to sell me 900,000 Eastern Mining. Do it through my Swiss nominee, same as our gold deals.'

'They've jumped this morning. Do I deal at any price?'

'Any price,' said Eddie. 'The higher the better. Do it through my Swiss account where you do the gold. And don't get involved personally.'

'Of course. I'll call you this evening.'

Back on the road he assessed his position. He was short of R800,000 worth of South African Mining and some R400,000 of Eastern Mining – and so far he was R100,000 down. The euphoric effects of the smoke were wearing off and he started to feel that cold fear in his stomach as he did when he took big market positions. If this one went wrong he was in no doubt about the outcome. He would be on the street with nothing. He looked at his watch. If he put his foot down he would be home for dinner. This was one deal he could not tell Lucy about.

36

Fred Spillman, Bill Borden and Jack Plane arrived at Kennedy airport to a heroes' welcome. Mark Ashford had seen to that. He had even arranged for the South African ambassador to be at the airport to meet them. Ashford never forgot the little touches – even when he was right on top.

The ambassador, Hendrik Coetzee, Ashford and his fellow directors stood on the tarmac waiting for the blue and gold South African Airways' Boeing 747 to taxi to a halt in front of them. They stood in the rain, beneath umbrellas, deafened by the screaming engines.

When they came down the steps, Ashford welcomed each man with handshakes and they posed for photographs, the ambassador strategically positioned in the middle of the group. Pressmen swarmed around them. Hendrik Coetzee felt distinctly uncomfortable. But he had his orders, and his diplomatic smile did not fade for a minute.

A motor-car cavalcade, headed by Mark Ashford's Cadillac, led the way to a celebration party on the fourth floor of the Waldorf, where two hundred financial journalists, brokers and analysts ate and drank the best the hotel had to offer. Mark Ashford was determined his victory was going to be a resounding one. He moved assiduously around the guests explaining to each one what an 'unfortunate mistake' it had all been. When the ambassador left after half an hour, Ashford made an enormous fuss of him at the door, in careful view of his guests.

After three hours, the party moved into its closing stages, and the toastmaster announced that SAM's chairman would say a few words. Mark stepped up onto a raised platform at one end of the banquet room and waited for the noise of the party to subside.

He lifted a glass of champagne. 'Fred . . . Bill . . . Jack, welcome home.' He drank and a drunken murmur of

'Welcome home' resounded round the room.

A scream of wailing sirens on the street below filled the silence that followed.

'Don't worry, Fred,' quipped Mark Ashford, 'they're not coming for you.'

Full of champagne and smoked salmon, the guests were ready to laugh at anything. Mark could not quieten the applause, catcalls, and wolf whistles for a full two minutes. The noise drowned the sirens outside.

'I must go, I have a plane waiting at the airport. But I want you all to stay and enjoy yourselves.'

He left through a side door, took the elevator down to the basement car park and drove out of a rear exit to the airport. He felt pretty good. His directors were home, the charges were dropped and he now owned most of Amanda. That morning the gold price had roared through $500 an ounce. He telephoned ahead to confirm he was on schedule for take off and ten minutes later the Cadillac turned into the private aircraft entrance to the airport and drew alongside SAM's yellow Lear Jet.

Ashford boarded, and went straight into his cabin to change for the flight into his favourite white towelling robe and slippers. He poured himself a large scotch and a few moments later he was strapped into his executive couch. The engines whined a pitch higher and slowly the jet taxied out onto the runway.

He looked out of the window; it was getting dark and the rain was sheeting across the oily tarmac. A flashing red light came out of the darkness. Fire or airport security, thought Mark. Then he noticed the light was coming straight towards them. Three other flashing lights followed behind.

He unclipped his belt and went through to the cockpit.

'Get out of here fast,' he yelled.

'But clearance hasn't . . .'

'Don't argue,' Mark threatened, 'just get us up in the air.'

The Lear's engines screamed and the plane gathered pace down the runway. Mark looked out of the window.

The flashing lights were much nearer. He could see quite clearly now – they were police cars, and closing fast.

He ducked back into the cockpit.

'Control has told us to stop,' said the pilot.

'Ignore them,' he yelled. 'Get us up.'

He dashed back to the window. The police car was alongside. The windows were down and a policeman was waving wildly for the plane to stop. The engines screamed and the plane vibrated lightly from its speed. They would be airborne any moment.

In disbelief Ashford saw a snub-nosed rifle jut out from the back window of the patrol car. It belched a volley of fire and smoke. He heard an explosion underneath him as one of the plane's tyres blew out, and the plane lurched to one side, throwing him against the cabin wall. Slowly, the jet ground to a halt. The pilot turned off the engines and the noise subsided, until all Mark could hear was the rain beating down on the roof.

The interior of the plane was lit with a blaze of fluorescent light and a loudspeaker boomed, 'You're surrounded. Come out slowly with your hands up.'

Ashford lifted himself clear of the debris and peered through the cabin window. Four police cars were drawn up in a semicircle with their headlights and roof lights trained on the plane. Police officers with long range rifles scrambled for cover behind squad cars. In the distance, two men carrying cameras scuttled out in the rain from the terminal building.

Mark scrambled down to the exit. He pulled down the handle, kicked open the door and released the switch to drop the steps.

He turned to the pilot. 'Follow me down. Don't say a word till the solicitors arrive.'

Slowly and uncertainly, Mark Ashford stepped through the cabin door into the blazing light.

37

The front page picture on the London *Financial Times* of Mark Ashford, dressed in white towelling gown and slippers, in front of his crippled Lear jet in the rain, hands held high and surrounded by rifle-aiming police, was enough for most fund managers. If they had hesitated after the arrests, they didn't now. They got out of South African Mining as if they had a charging bull behind them.

SAM shares didn't just fall – they crashed. A frenzy of selling hit the New York market in the last ten minutes of trading before the market closed on Monday as news of Mark Ashford's arrest spread round Wall Street. The shares dropped from $9 to $6¼ when trading was halted.

London was next. SAM shares plummeted from £6 to £4 on the first bargain of the day. The jobbers in the market who bought and sold SAM's shares had their pitch swarming with sellers. There wasn't a buyer in sight.

An hour later, the Johannesburg market opened. Pierre Bouchard called Eddie the night before and Eddie gave him his instructions. Eddie and Izzie met briefly in Izzie's ramshackle office shortly before the market opened.

Eddie hardly dare ask how Izzie was going to deal.

'Suppose you'll buy them back first thing,' he mentioned casually. Izzie didn't answer. His brown hooded eyes glared with anger at Eddie.

'Where will you be?' he asked.

'They won't let me on the floor; but I suppose I'm allowed in the public gallery.'

'OK,' said Izzie, checking his watch, 'let's get over there.'

Ten minutes later, as soon as the big doors at the end of the exchange were opened, Izzie marched across the trading floor grinning good-naturedly. This was one morning's trade he was going to enjoy.

'South African Mining,' he bellowed above the growing hubbub of deals being done at the beginning of the day.

Max Llewellyn's head dealer stepped forward, Izzie sold him fifty thousand shares at eight rand.

'Tell Max if he's going to support the price of this shit, he'd better get his cheque book out. There's a lot more where this came from.' The dealer left without a word.

'Seller SAM,' yelled Izzie. Then he started bidding the stock down on the prices board. Heads turned towards him as he bid lower and lower.

Up in the public gallery, overhanging one end of the exchange, Eddie watched closely as a crowd gathered round. Izzie's trading antics never failed to entertain.

'Come on you bastards, buy some of this shit,' Izzie shouted.

Max Llewellyn bounded out onto the floor, his face tight and worried. He came over to the crowd. Izzie gave him a cold ruthless stare and cleared his throat loudly, as if to spit. He didn't, but Max got the message.

'South African Mining, seller,' yelled Izzie again as Max stomped away.

Izzie swung round to the other dealers waving his arms. 'If it's good enough for the president's firm to buy, it's good enough for you bastards,' he roared.

Two other dealers joined him and started calling SAM shares lower.

Max Llewellyn returned. 'How many have you got?'

'To you – a hundred thousand,' snapped Izzie.

Max blanched. He had been told to support the price but R600,000 in one chunk was a lot.

'I'll take 25,000 and watch the price.'

'You can take the lot – or nothing, Mr President.'

Max stared at him blankly.

'Go and ask Mark Ashford to increase your buying limit – or have they locked him up?' Llewellyn turned on his heel and left without a word.

More dealers joined Izzie as sellers of SAM, and the price started to slide. Then there were seven of them. Llewellyn's head dealer picked up small parcels of stock from each one, but the weight of selling was just too great. Izzie stood firmly in the middle of the group stamping his foot and shouting 'Seller, South African Mining'. The price slid from eight rand straight down to six rand and didn't steady up till it reached four rand. Izzie knew the other dealers and guessed their clients were institutions.

'Dumping many?' he asked one.

'Nearly 500,000. They're never going to get rid of them.'

At four rands a share, Izzie left the group and went over to his desk. He made two phone calls and returned, still shouting with the others to sell SAM shares.

Moments later, two dealers arrived on the floor bidding for SAM shares. In four minutes, they bought 470,000 of them. They bought from everybody except Izzie. There were still plenty on offer, but the price had moved up to 4.50 rand. Shortly after they left the floor, Izzie met them for a drink in the first-floor members' bar. The shares were rebooked to Izzie, a R10,000 commission was paid to each of them and he and Eddie had bought back all the shares they 'shorted'.

Izzie walked back into the market to check the prices board. SAM were trading at five rands. Most of the dealers selling had left the floor and Max Llewellyn's head dealer was negotiating with two that remained.

Good, he had caught the bottom of the market. That gave Izzie immense satisfaction. It wasn't the rewards of the game that counted. What mattered to Izzie was how well he played. Getting it right was much more important these days than the money.

He strode across the floor to the doors at the end of the exchange. As he passed under the public gallery he looked up at the glass front and saw the gallery was empty.

Eddie was waiting for him outside.

'You've bought 200,000 at four rand,' said Izzie, his eyes sparkling.

Eddie did the calculation. Two hundred thousand at an average price of eight rand a share made him R800,000. Add in the R300,000 Pierre made in New York and he was R1.1 million richer.

'Looks like I'm back in business.'

'Congratulations, man.'

'Thanks,' said Eddie, beaming. He pulled Izzie lightly by the shoulder. 'Come on, I'm buying you lunch.'

They burst through the door of Madame Sikorsky's crowded restaurant in high spirits, and almost collided with the *grande madame*.

'The most beautiful woman in the world,' exclaimed Izzie, holding his arms out towards her.

'Darling,' said Madame Sikorsky, pushing her outsized bust and plunging neckline towards him. 'If I ever left home, it would be for a lion like you.' She planted an ostentatious kiss on Izzie's cheek, laughed, and put her arm round him.

A waiter walked past with a bottle of champagne in a silver bucket. 'Just what we want,' said Eddie, plucking the bottle from the ice.

'That's my table,' said Izzie scornfully pointing to the corner table. 'What are they doing there?'

Madame Sikorsky moved swiftly. She made an excuse and the couple moved elsewhere.

Eddie and Izzie sat down and Madame Sikorsky brought the glasses. Eddie popped the cork and watched the sparkling liquid bubble over the side.

He stood up and handed his glass to Madame Sikorsky. 'This one is for you, my darling,' he said kissing her hand.

'My goodness,' said Madame Sikorsky. 'What's the celebration?'

Izzie inclined his head across the table. 'Blue eyes here has just made a million.'

She never knew whether Izzie was being serious. 'Darling, how wonderful,' she drained her glass in one gulp, kissed Eddie on the cheek and departed.

Jock McCullough's straight, dapper figure strode across the restaurant and stopped at Eddie's table.

'Well done, Eddie, I've heard the news,' he said holding out his huge right hand, the wafer thin Piaget tightly stretched round his massive wrist.

Eddie stood up and shook hands.

'Thanks. Won't you have a drink?'

'Not now,' he said glancing at Izzie.

'Do you know Izzie Van Royen?'

'Yes, Jock and I are old pals,' said Izzie dryly, and drained his glass.

'Pals might be overstating the case,' McCullough winked. 'We crossed swords way back.'

'Well,' Eddie said lightly. 'If I'd been smart I would have sold when you did.'

'Glad you didn't,' smiled McCullough. 'I would never have seen Mark Ashford in his dressing gown.' He turned to go.

'Come and have lunch with me. Ring my secretary and tell her when you're free.'

'Thanks. I'll do that.'

Eddie sat down. 'What happened between you two?'

'Not now,' said Izzie pushing his empty glass across the table. 'Why spoil a good lunch?'

Eddie poured more champagne and changed the subject. 'So we beat the bastard.'

'Not really,' said Izzie philosophically. 'He'll find a way out.'

'Well we made ourselves some money.'

'That we did,' chuckled Izzie. 'What are you going to do now?'

'Haven't really thought. I'd like to stay here but I'm barred from the market. I may go to America, maybe London.'

'Why don't you come in with me? You could have my back office, I could do all your dealing. I'm sure you could get some clients back.'

'Do you think we'd get on?'

'It hasn't been too bad so far. You're not bound in any way. You could leave whenever you wanted. It might work out. I need someone in the office and you need someone in the market – even if it's just to buy your own shares.'

Izzie downed his glass of champagne.

'You know Eddie, there's another stock we should look at. Max Llewellyn and his cronies have been . . .'

Eddie banged the table top with the palm of his hand. 'No way,' he laughed. 'At least not for a month. I'm taking

Lucy and the girls off somewhere quiet.' Eddie saw a flicker of disappointment in Izzie's face. 'We'll take a raincheck on it till I get back,' he told him.

Izzie topped up the glasses. 'Well, I'm glad it all worked out for you. When you started 'shorting' all those shares, I didn't think you were going to make it.'

'You know something,' grinned Eddie, 'I didn't think I would either.'

Other Arrow Books of interest:

MONTE CARLO

Stephen Sheppard

It is May 1940 when Harry Pilikian, a young American, drives his Rolls Royce through the French night. By the time he reaches the principality of Monaco, the Germans have invaded France – and the war begins in earnest.

In neutral Monte Carlo, for the next two years, an uncertain peace prevails. The Italian army pays a token visit, Gestapo men move about in plain clothes, and refugees from all parts of the world – the rich, beautiful and bizarre – gather to sit out the war in safety and comfort.

But amidst the glitter and elegance of this famous resort, the menace of engulfing war is never far away. And those who fled to Monte Carlo for sanctuary are inescapably drawn into the anguish and horror of the conflict . . .

GHOST FLIGHT

William Katz

One second there were six dots floating gently across the radar-scope – then, suddenly, there were seven. It was a twin-prop, pre-war Lockheed Electra, and it cut across the sky, a phantom plane, heading for the LA airport, weaving between the waiting jets as though it owned the air. The pilot looked down. My God, she thought, it's changed so much. But still it was America. Seven presidents later – but home. Home at last.

GHOST FLIGHT

Out of nowhere and out of decades, Amelia Earhart returns – from the year 1937 and from a mission she never completed. Her homecoming is the start of a nightmare. For with her comes alive again the evil of the past. The past of screaming demons and bloody ghosts, of an unspeakable evil that had never died – but had slept and waited . . .

£1.75

NILE

Laurie Devine

Egypt . . . and a small Muslim village where life has remained almost unchanged since the time of the Pharaohs. It is a world of fear, danger, and magic. But most fearful and dangerous of all is a woman who violates the ancient taboos. A woman such as Mona . . .

Meanwhile, in the sleek westernized world of Alexandria, Youssef al-Masri is growing up in a rich, powerful Arab-Jewish family. He seems destined for a life of wealth – or dissipation.

Until he and Mona meet and fall in love . . . and until history tears their world apart.

And for two generations their children and their children's children will try to repair that fatal rift.

Nile is a superb epic of high romance set against a background of seductive richness.

BESTSELLING FICTION FROM ARROW

All these books are available from your bookshop or news-agent or you can order them direct. Just tick the titles you want and complete the form below.

☐	THE COMPANY OF SAINTS	Evelyn Anthony	£1.95
☐	HESTER DARK	Emma Blair	£1.95
☐	1985	Anthony Burgess	£1.75
☐	2001: A SPACE ODYSSEY	Arthur C. Clarke	£1.75
☐	NILE	Laurie Devine	£2.75
☐	THE BILLION DOLLAR KILLING	Paul Erdman	£1.75
☐	THE YEAR OF THE FRENCH	Thomas Flanagan	£2.50
☐	LISA LOGAN	Marie Joseph	£1.95
☐	SCORPION	Andrew Kaplan	£2.50
☐	SUCCESS TO THE BRAVE	Alexander Kent	£1.95
☐	STRUMPET CITY	James Plunkett	£2.95
☐	FAMILY CHORUS	Claire Rayner	£2.50
☐	BADGE OF GLORY	Douglas Reeman	£1.95
☐	THE KILLING DOLL	Ruth Rendell	£1.95
☐	SCENT OF FEAR	Margaret Yorke	£1.75

Postage _____

Total _____

ARROW BOOKS, BOOKSERVICE BY POST, PO BOX 29, DOUGLAS, ISLE OF MAN, BRITISH ISLES

Please enclose a cheque or postal order made out to Arrow Books Limited for the amount due including 15p per book for postage and packing both for orders within the UK and for overseas orders.

Please print clearly

NAME...

ADDRESS..

....

Whilst every effort is made to keep prices down and to keep popular books in print, Arrow Books cannot guarantee that prices will be the same as those advertised here or that the books will be available.